What Eric Knew

Atheneum Books by James Howe

WHAT ERIC KNEW

A Sebastian Barth Mystery by

JAMES HOWE

Atheneum   *New York*

Library of Congress Cataloging in Publication Data

Howe, James.   What Eric knew.

(Sebastian Barth mysteries; bk. 1)
SUMMARY: After Eric moves away he sends cryptic notes
to Sebastian and David, who follow them
to investigate a mysterious death.
1. Children's stories, American. [1. Mystery and
detective stories] I. Title. II. Series.
PZ7.H83727Wh   1985   [Fic]   85-7418
ISBN 0-689-31702-6

Atheneum
Macmillan Publishing Company
866 Third Avenue
New York, NY 10022

Type set by Heritage Printers, Charlotte,
North Carolina
Printed and bound by Fairfield Graphics, Fairfield,
Pennsylvania
Designed by Mary Ahern

Printed in the United States of America

10 9 8 7 6 5 4 3

To
Melissa Whitcraft
&
Steven Mintz

What Eric Knew

1 THE FIRST THING Sebastian Barth heard when he woke that summer morning was mail being pushed through the slot in the front door and landing with a soft thud inside. From the sound, it was a two-magazine day, he decided. He yawned and rolled over in bed. The clock read ten past nine. Sebastian smiled at the luxury of sleeping so late.

Stretching, he reached for his robe and headed downstairs. The house was still. His father had probably left for the radio station at least an hour before. And his mother would be at the farmers' market buying fresh vegetables for her restaurant. As for Gram, he couldn't guess where she was this morning. Sebastian's grandmother had so many "worthy causes," as she called them, that "there weren't enough hours in the day."

When he entered the kitchen, his two cats, Boo and Chopped Liver, attacked his ankles and purred loudly.

"Give me a break, you guys," he said. "You've been fed already."

Chopped Liver flashed him a we-won't-tell-anybody-if-you-feed-us-again sort of look, but Sebastian

[3]

just shook his head and poured himself a bowl of cereal.

A newspaper lay open on the kitchen table. He noticed a story about some rare books being stolen from a library in New Haven, read about half of it, and turned to the comics.

The phone rang.

"Hey, it's you."

Sebastian recognized the voice of his best friend, David, who lived across the street. "Were you expecting a wrong number?" he asked.

"I didn't think you'd be back from your route yet. You coming over?"

"I didn't have to do my route today. And sure I'm coming over. How was the game?"

"Good. What do you want to do today?"

"I don't know. What do you want to do?"

"I don't know. You want to do some biking?"

"Maybe. But right now I want to rescue my cereal from terminal sogginess. I'll be over in a half hour."

"Okay," David said. And then, as Sebastian was about to hang up, he added, "It's been kind of quiet around here since Eric moved, hasn't it?"

"Yeah," Sebastian said. "Eric did have a way of keeping things lively. At least he did before . . . you know."

"Yeah. Well, see you later."

"See you later."

After he hung up the phone, Sebastian remembered the mail. He'd been right. There were two magazines. There was also something for him. The thin envelope showed no return address, just a Boston postmark. And inside was the strangest letter he had ever received.

2 SEBASTIAN showed the letter to David. It read, "S.I.S."

"That's it?"

Sebastian nodded.

"Who's it from? Wait, don't tell me—Eric, of course."

The two boys were walking down Chestnut Street, toward the house where Eric used to live.

"But what's it mean?" David asked, when Sebastian remained silent. "Hey, look. Someone's moved in."

"I know. I met them yesterday when you were at the game. There's a kid our age."

David regarded Eric's old house with new interest. "What's he like?" he asked.

"You'll see."

A slim woman with short, gray hair stood on the front porch of the house calling, "Buster! Buster!"

"Buster!" David snorted. "What kind of name is that? Gee, Sebastian, that's not the kid, is it? Buster?"

"Don't worry," said Sebastian, as a child ran past them and into the yard, "you won't become the laughingstock of Pembroke because you've got a friend named Buster. That's the kid's little brother. *That's* the kid."

Sebastian pointed toward the garage next to the house. Someone in shorts and a halter top was hosing down a garbage pail.

"A girl?" David said incredulously. The new kid waved and ran toward them. "You didn't tell me...oh, great. Just what we need, a *girl*." He made a fist and said, "Curse you, Eric Mather."

"Hi," said the girl, as her sneakers brought her to a squeaky halt. She had a thicket of red hair and a face busy with freckles. When she smiled at Sebastian, her braces sparkled.

"Hi," said Sebastian. "This is my friend, David Lepinsky."

David mumbled something.

"And this is Corrie...."

"Wingate," said Corrie. "Hi, David. What are you guys up to?"

"Well, actually," said Sebastian, "we've got a mystery on our hands. Or sort of a mystery, anyway." Sebastian gave Corrie Eric's letter.

"What are you *doing*?" David hissed.

[7]

"Relax. She's okay."

"What's it mean?" Corrie asked, handing the letter back to Sebastian.

"I'm not sure, but I have a hunch."

"Sebastian always has a hunch," David said.

"I think it has something to do with the way Eric was acting before he left."

"Eric? Oh yeah, the kid who used to live here." Corrie picked at a mosquito bite on her leg. "How was he acting?"

"Weird," said Sebastian.

David nodded. "Definitely weird," he said.

Sebastian went on, "Eric was always . . . well, adventurous, I guess you could say. He liked . . ."

"Getting into trouble," David said.

"Something like that. He liked having a good time, goofing around, nosing into other people's business. You know?"

"I think so. But what's weird about that?"

"Nothing. It's just that he changed a few weeks before he moved. All of a sudden, he got kind of quiet and kept to himself. When we asked him what was going on, he didn't want to talk about it. Said he *couldn't* talk about it. And then, about three days before he moved, he fell down a flight of stairs and broke his leg."

"Wow," said Corrie, as her picking drew blood. "How come?"

"How come what?" asked David.

"How come he fell down the stairs?"

"We don't know," Sebastian said. "He wouldn't tell us. But he hinted that he'd been pushed."

"Wow," Corrie said again.

"And now this," said Sebastian, holding up Eric's letter. "S.I.S."

"Are they somebody's initials?"

"Seems like it," Sebastian said.

"But we don't know anybody with those initials," said David.

"Well, I can think of one person." Sebastian paused and then said, "Susan Iris Siddons."

David looked at him as if he'd gone nuts.

"And you think maybe it was Susan Siddons who pushed Eric down the stairs?" asked Corrie.

"I have a hunch that's what Eric's trying to tell us," Sebastian said. "There's just one little problem."

"Definitely," said David.

"What?" Corrie asked.

Sebastian looked past Corrie's house to the cemetery in its shadow. "Susan Siddons died in 1902," he said.

3

SUSAN IRIS SIDDONS

DIED

AUGUST 10. 1902.

AGED 49 YEARS.

In life did I reap much pain,
In death greater pain I sow.
'Tis a garden of poison'd ivy,
And the roots lie here below.

"SHE WASN'T a very happy woman," Corrie Wingate said.

"Sharp observation," said Sebastian.

"Well, for starters," David said, "she couldn't have been too thrilled to kick the bucket at forty-nine."

"She probably didn't *know* she was going to die," Corrie said.

"Oh, but she did," said Sebastian. "She'd been sick a long time."

Corrie shuddered and walked away from the gravestone with its odd epitaph. "This place is creepy," she said. Then, over her shoulder, she asked, "How do you know so much about somebody who died in 1902, anyway?"

"Susan Siddons is a Pembroke legend," said David. "Her ghost is still around, you know."

Corrie turned to face the boys. "Great," she said, "not only do I get to live next door to a cemetery, but I have ghosts for neighbors. I should have stayed in Troy."

"It's not just that. The Siddons family is famous. Didn't you ever hear of Siddons College?"

"Of course," Corrie replied, in a way that made Sebastian fairly certain she never had.

"Well, Siddons College was founded by Cornelius Siddons. Susan was his wife. It's hard to live in Pembroke and *not* know about the Siddons family. Besides, they still live here."

"So you told me," Corrie said, with a nod back to Susan Siddons's grave.

Sebastian smiled. "Not just ghosts," he said. "*Real* people, too. Ricky Siddons is a friend of ours."

"He was Eric's best friend," said David.

"His brother Danny rings the bell."

"What bell?"

[11]

Sebastian indicated the steeple of the church the other side of the cemetery. "That one. Every night at nine a member of the Siddons family rings it."

David said, "Another legend."

"And the legend of the ghost?" Corrie asked.

"I don't know the whole story," Sebastian said. "Something to do with a ring she left behind. I know someone we can ask if you want to know more. Someone who swears he's seen the ghost."

"Well, don't *you* want to know more?" asked Corrie. "I mean, isn't this ghost supposed to have something to do with your friend Eric?"

Sebastian nodded. "Let's go up to the station and talk to Uncle Harry," he said. "It's kind of a long walk. We could take our bikes."

"Let's walk," said Corrie.

As they passed through the cemetery, Corrie said, almost in a whisper, "Did you ever notice how cemeteries squish?"

David and Sebastian looked at her.

"I mean, the ground's all soft and bumpy. It makes me feel like I'm walking on bones and rotting flesh."

David and Sebastian looked at each other.

"Listen to this one," Corrie called suddenly. She read from a tipped gravestone, " 'Captain Joseph Piper.' Gee, he was only twenty-seven when he died. 'Stop, careless stranger, pass not by. Pause and reflect that thou must die. Remember I was once like thee, and what I am thou soon must be.' "

Corrie gazed at the stone a moment longer. Her cheeks felt hot. "Let's get out of here," she said. "This place gives me the willies."

"I'd believe you," said Sebastian, "if you didn't look like you were enjoying it so much."

Corrie smiled at Sebastian and felt her cheeks grow hotter.

4 HARRY DOBBS had been at radio station WEB-FM for more years than anyone could remember. He often joked that the only ones there with more seniority were the magazines in the reception area. He was a friendly polar bear, pink and white and large. Between his thick, white mustache and his laughing blue eyes ran a network of blood vessels resembling a road map. "The map of my past, present, and future," he called his face.

"Somebody else asked me about Susan Siddons recently," said Harry Dobbs, sending a smoke ring into the already stale air of Studio B. "Well, now, I'll tell you this—that is one restless lady."

"What do you mean?" asked Corrie.

"What do I mean? She won't take her nap like a good girl, that's what I mean. Always getting up and wandering about where she doesn't belong. And, I don't mind saying, scaring the whoopsies out of people while she's at it."

"You're not putting us on, are you, Uncle Harry?" said Sebastian.

"Sebastian," Harry replied solemnly, "you know me better than that. I don't put people on." He

[14]

crushed the life out of his cigarette in a milk-glass ashtray. "In fact," he went on, "I wouldn't be saying any of this if I hadn't seen the lady myself."

Corrie glanced at Sebastian and David to see whether or not they were laughing. They weren't. She noticed that David held a small, spiral notebook in his lap.

"It was around dusk, as I remember. Just about this time of year. Yes, July it was. July. I was out walking Fibber. You remember Fibber, Sebastian. Well, I had taken the old boy for a walk up near the Siddons house. Now, it's usually pretty quiet up there, but that night it was so still, even the crickets held their breaths. All of a sudden, old Fibber started to bark. Well, I jumped, I'll tell you. And then I started to laugh. At myself, you know, for jumping like that. 'What's the matter, boy?' I said. 'Something spook you?' Well, Fibber, he just kept on barking. And when I saw what he was barking at, it spooked me too. Plenty. There, taking a stroll through the garden, was the ghost of Susan Siddons. As clear to me then as you are to me now. I could hardly believe my eyes."

"So why did you?"

The question startled Harry. Then, seeing it was Sebastian who asked it, he laughed. "Well, I didn't at first," he said. "I shook my head and told myself it was somebody dressed up to look like her. I'd always heard that Susan Siddons favored big-brimmed hats. And whoever this was was wearing a big-brimmed hat; black it was, with a veil. That wasn't what convinced me, though, nor the fact that she was wearing a long, black dress when long dresses hadn't been the fashion for many a year. No, it was something else . . . and something *else* . . . that convinced me it was Susan Siddons. First, there was that white glove. She wore just one white glove. One hand she kept bare, you see, so that when she found the ring that belonged to her, she'd be able to slip it right on her finger."

"The ring," Corrie said. "Sebastian said something about that. Mr. Dobbs—"

"Oh, now, if we're to be friends, Corrie, I won't have you calling me Mr. Dobbs. I'm Uncle Harry. At least to the young folks I am. Why, even Sebastian's dad called me that when he was a tad."

Corrie smiled. "Uncle Harry," she said, "what's the legend of the ring?"

Harry coughed and reached for another cigarette. "Cornelius Siddons married again a year and a day after Susan's death. Jenny her name was. She was a nurse. Now, it seems that Cornelius gave this Jenny his first wife's wedding ring. And Susan, or her ghost, I should say, was so unhappy about it that she appeared to Jenny on her wedding night and demanded that she hand it over. Terrified, Jenny ran from the room and hid the ring. And never, from that day to this, has that ring been seen again. Jenny never wore it. And no one has ever found it. Not man nor woman nor ghost. I don't know that anyone is still looking for it—anyone besides Susan Siddons, that is. And that's why she still walks the earth and why she wears just one glove."

"And something else?" asked Sebastian.

"Hmm?"

"You said there was something else, and something else, that convinced you it was Susan Siddons. First, there was the white glove. And then. . . ."

"Ah, yes, yes. Well, then there was this. When I saw her, I let go of Fibber's leash, and he chased up the hill after her. Now what would a normal person do when she hears a barking dog coming at her? Turn? Run? Cry out? She didn't do any of those things, my friends. No, she did something only a ghost would do. She vanished. Not in a puff of smoke, mind. Nothing as dramatic as that. In fact, I'm sure I couldn't tell you how she did it. All I know is that when Fibber reached the spot where she'd been standing, she was no longer there."

A clear, metallic voice sliced through the smoky air and said, "Five minutes, Harry."

"Right you are," Harry boomed.

There was a tap on the studio window. Two ancient, birdlike women beamed at Harry through masks of white powder and red rouge. When they smiled, their top front teeth fell forward in unison. Sebastian could almost hear the slippery slide and click as the partial plates were sucked back into place. They waved wispy handkerchiefs, and Harry waved back.

"Ah, the Braddock sisters," he said, smiling. Then he winked at Corrie and said, "My groupies."

5 "FIDDLE-FADDLE!" exclaimed Jessica Hallem.

Sebastian's grandmother was seated on the white wicker loveseat doing needlepoint. Sebastian sat beside her. Across from them, David rocked back and forth in the matching wicker rocker. Corrie, cross-legged on a floor pillow, attempted to seduce one of Sebastian's cats into playing. But Boo was not about to be won over by someone so new to the neighborhood. Besides, he was too busy flicking his tail in and out of the rocker's to-and-fro.

"Harry Dobbs is a fool, Sebastian. And he's just the kind of fool that'll tell stories to hear the sound of his own voice."

"But, Gram—"

"You asked me what I thought, and I'm telling you."

"I asked you what you thought of the ghost story, not what you thought of Uncle Harry."

Jessica gave Sebastian one of her looks.

There was a loud screech. Either Boo or David had changed his rhythm. Boo left the room, wounded and indignant. David stopped rocking and spoke.

"I've been doing some reading about ghosts, Mrs. Hallem," he said, "and, according to researchers, everything that Uncle Harry told us could have really happened. They say that there's no proof that ghosts—well, they call them apparitions, actually—there's no proof that they don't exist."

"And there's no proof that they *do*," said Jessica Hallem. "You can do all the reading you like, David, but it's all theory and speculation. As far as anyone *knows*—anyone more reliable than Harry Dobbs, that is—there are no such things as ghosts."

"Apparitions," said David.

"Whatever," said Jessica. "I have done a great deal of research, too, you know. In my work with the historical society, I have studied the Siddons family thoroughly. And I can assure you there isn't a skeleton to be found in their closets. Or a ghost in their garden, for that matter. Oh, New Englanders must have their legends, to be sure. And we have ours about Susan Siddons and her lost ring. But legends are for tourists, David. And, though you haven't lived in Pembroke all your life, you are *not*, I trust, a tourist."

The subject was closed.

David rocked back in his chair as silence and Boo returned to the room. The cat regarded the chair with squint-eyed contempt and jumped up onto Sebastian's lap. Corrie drew her knees to her chin, wrapped her arms around them, and noticed that both the cat and Sebastian had green eyes flecked with gold.

A comfortable quiet settled over the room like a warm, familiar blanket. It had been a tiring day. After talking with Harry Dobbs, Sebastian and David had shown Corrie around the radio station and introduced her to Sebastian's father, who was the station manager. Then they had gone back to Corrie's house to help the Wingates with their unpacking and share an impromptu supper of pizza and salad. Now they were content to listen to the chirping of crickets and the occasional whoosh of a passing car. No one felt the need to speak. No one did again until the church bell chimed.

"Nine o'clock," said Sebastian, after the bell had rung twice.

"Listen," said Jessica, putting down her needlepoint. There was a moment's silence. Then the bell rang again. And once again.

"What is that boy up to?" Jessica said with a scowl. "That's not the way it's done. As a Siddons, he should know that. But as a Siddons, he will do as he pleases, I expect. And no one will say boo."

The cat lifted his head.

Corrie did not know what to make of Jessica Hallem's words or her scowl.

She thought about them later that night as she looked out of her bedroom window at the church steeple. The bell was in clear silhouette against the moonlit sky. Just as she was about to turn away, she noticed a shifting of shadows in the cemetery below. Someone was there. Someone dressed in black. All in black.

Except for one white glove.

6 THE NEWSPAPER landed on the second step.

"Not bad," Sebastian said to himself. He picked up speed and turned the corner. There he came upon Corrie Wingate and her father, jogging.

"Good morning, Reverend Wingate. Hi, Corrie."

The two joggers looked back over their shoulders. "Well, good morning, Sebastian," said Drew Wingate. His face was red and wet. His glasses were fogged over. Sebastian wondered how he kept from bumping into trees.

"Sebastian," Corrie called. "I have something to tell you. Something important."

"So tell me," Sebastian said, tossing a newspaper. It landed on the porch. "Way to go," he said.

"Not now," said Corrie. "In private."

"What's this?" said her father. "My little girl has something to tell a boy that she can't say in front of her old dad? I thought *I* was your boyfriend, Peaches."

Corrie said, "Daddy." It was a warning.

"Listen," said Sebastian, "I'm almost through

with my route. When you finish jogging, meet me at David's house. It's the one right across the street from mine. We can talk there."

"But I have to eat breakfast."

"You can eat at David's. Josh—that's David's dad—always makes enough breakfast for an army."

"But—"

"Don't worry. He likes crowds. I think it's because he works alone all day. I'll see you there."

Sebastian threw his last newspaper. It landed in a bush.

7 "HEY, JOSH," Sebastian called through the screen door. "What's Flinch up to these days?" He dropped his bike and bounded up the backporch steps.

Josh Lepinsky was making blueberry pancakes. When he wasn't making blueberry pancakes, he wrote murder mysteries featuring a New York City cop named Flinch. He had written seven books in the series thus far and was almost famous.

"He's on a homicide case," Josh said. "A proper young lady from Scarsdale with a fondness for heroin."

"I guess she wasn't all that proper," Sebastian said.

"Certainly not when last seen."

"Where was that?"

"Face down in the trunk of a Toyota Corolla."

Sebastian nodded and hijacked a blueberry. "A *proper* young lady would have been found in a Mercedes 380 SL," he said.

"Appearances can be deceiving," said Josh.

David entered the kitchen, rubbing sleep from his eyes.

"I thought I heard your voice," he said to Sebastian. "Mooching breakfast off the neighbors again, huh?"

"Yep. I even invited a friend. I hope that's okay, Josh."

"Sebastian, any friend of yours, et cetera."

"What friend?" David asked.

There was a knock on the front door. "Sebastian?" called a feminine voice.

"*Her?*" David said.

Sebastian nodded.

"Why'd you invite *her* here?"

Josh said, "Something wrong with her?"

"No," said Sebastian. "Other than being a girl." On his way out, he turned to David and said, "Don't worry. It isn't catching."

"What have you got against girls?" Josh asked his son.

"Nothing," David mumbled. "They're just so ... so ...."

"Good morning, everyone. Please, don't get up. No, no, I'm sorry. No autographs before breakfast. I'm simply not myself until I've had my glass of o.j."

David's kid sister, Rachel, entered the room. She wore Miss Piggy pajamas, rhinestone-studded sunglasses, and a blonde wig.

"I rest my case," said David.

"Josh, this is Corrie," said Sebastian from the

kitchen doorway. "She just moved into Eric's house. Her dad's the new minister at First Church."

Josh turned, dripping batter on the linoleum. "It's nice to meet you, Corrie. I'll try not to judge you by the company you keep."

Corrie smiled at Josh.

Rachel extended her hand. "Hello," she said. "I'm Barbra Streisand."

After breakfast, Josh left the kids to clean up while he went to his study to work. Rachel announced that she'd be unable to help with the dishes as she would simply die without a shower. David told her she was making it a difficult decision for him but agreed to let her go.

"Look," Corrie said when they were alone, "I don't know if it was *really* the ghost of Susan Siddons. I mean, before yesterday, I didn't even believe in ghosts. Now I'm *seeing* them."

"What did she do exactly?" asked Sebastian.

"When I first saw her, she was standing near the grave—*her* grave. At least, I think that's where she was. Then she walked toward the church. It was hard to see her clearly because she was all in black. Except for the glove, of course. That's what I kept my eye on. But then, when she was almost to the church, she . . . well, she . . ."

David set down the glass he was wiping and looked at Corrie. Sebastian had not taken his eyes off her since she'd begun speaking moments earlier.

"She disappeared," said Corrie.

The warbling of a wet nine-year-old drifted through the kitchen ceiling.

"Memories . . . may be beautiful and yet. . . ."

"This is crazy," David said. "How do we investigate a ghost?"

"I think we start with people," said Sebastian. "And hope that they lead us to the ghost."

"People, people who need people. . . ."

"And I know just the one to talk to first," Sebastian said. "Let's go."

As Sebastian, David, and Corrie passed by the staircase, Rachel appeared on the landing above. She wore a floor-length white towel and clutched a toilet plunger to her chest. Looking down at her brother and his friends, she said, "I want to thank the members of the Academy for this award."

8 "I DON'T KNOW any more than you do,"
said Ricky Siddons.

"Oh, come on," David said. "You and
Eric were best friends. He must have told you stuff."

"And I'm saying he didn't."

Ricky slipped another quarter into the hungry
mouth of the arcade game. Corrie and David watched
the screen battle while Sebastian watched Ricky's
face. Concentration wrinkled it like an old peach.

Sebastian waited to speak until Ricky had finished his campaign against the aliens. "Listen," he
said, "it wasn't like Eric to clam up. If he wasn't talking to us, he must have been talking to someone."

Ricky shrugged and walked to the snack stand.
The others followed. "Maybe," he said, "but he
wasn't talking to me."

"Did he ever say anything about Susan Siddons?" Corrie asked.

Ricky's face was blank. Then he turned to Corrie and almost smiled. "Now that you mention it,"
he said, "I think he did say something about her.
Something about a ring, I think. Does that make
sense?"

[29]

Corrie and Sebastian and David looked at one another. Corrie was about to respond when Sebastian cut her off.

"Not really," he said to Ricky. "Does it make sense to you?"

Ricky shrugged again. He was good at shrugging. "Nope," he said. He ordered a cherry Coke and picked up a magazine and said not another word.

"Gosh," Corrie said outside the arcade, "I thought you said he was a friend of yours. He sure has a funny way of showing it."

"He's a funny guy," said Sebastian.

David was writing in his notebook.

"There's one thing I don't understand," Corrie said. "He didn't seem to make the connection between Susan Siddons and the ring. If everybody else in town knows about it, wouldn't he?"

"You'd think so," said Sebastian. "But, of course, there's a simple reason why he didn't."

Corrie looked at him.

"He was lying."

"How do you know?"

"He just *knows*," said David, shoving his notebook into a pocket. "Sebastian reads people the way I read books."

"He's been avoiding us the way Eric did," Sebastian said. "Ricky's stuck-up, but he doesn't avoid people. Besides, there's no way he wouldn't know about the ring. He's a Siddons, after all."

"Do you think he and Eric were in on something?" Corrie asked.

"Maybe," Sebastian replied. "One thing's for sure. Whatever Eric knew, Ricky knows too. And Ricky isn't talking."

"But if they didn't want you guys to know about it, why would Eric send you that note?"

Sebastian stopped walking and looked at Corrie. "That's a good question. I'll have to think about it. But my hunch is that whatever it was wasn't safe for Eric to talk about while he was still living here."

"Then why not just write and tell you the whole thing?"

"Maybe he's afraid," said Sebastian.

"Afraid?" David said. "Afraid of what?"

"That's what we have to find out. That, and whether what he's afraid of is some*thing*. Or some-*one*."

Turning to Corrie, Sebastian said, "When Eric lived here, the three of us investigated mysteries all the time. David and I liked it because it was fun trying to figure things out. Eric liked it because it was dangerous. He was always pushing us to do things our common sense told us not to. Before he moved, he might have been investigating a mystery on his own. Maybe it was something *really* dangerous, something he didn't want us in on because he was afraid we'd get hurt. Then *he* got hurt—pushed down the stairs because he knew too much. Now, he wants us

[3 1]

to take over the investigation because, dangerous or not, it's something really important."

"And maybe," said David, "S.I.S. stands for Sebastian Is a Sucker. Maybe Eric is putting us on."

Sebastian thought a moment and said, "Maybe."

When the kids got to Sebastian's house, a letter was waiting. It was from Eric, and it read, "In the tower."

9 "ARE YOU SURE this is the tower he meant?" Corrie asked.

Even though she was used to scrambling around the insides of churches, First Church was still new to Corrie, and its tower staircase unfamiliar.

"There aren't that many towers in Pembroke," said Sebastian. "Besides, we used to hang out up here sometimes. I'm sure this is what Eric meant."

"I just wish I knew what we were looking for," David said.

The small room at the top of the stairs was divided into darkness and light. In the darkness were Sebastian, David, and Corrie. In the single shaft of sunlight was a rope. It was swaying.

"Is this the hanging room?" Corrie asked.

"That's the bell rope," said David.

"I know that. I was making a joke. I do that when I'm scared."

"Girls," David muttered. Then to Corrie he said, "You're not scared of the dark, are you?"

"No, but I'll tell you what I *am* scared of. I'm scared of whatever's making that rope move. In case you haven't noticed, there's no wind in here."

[33]

Sebastian flicked on the lights. A body was slumped in a corner.

"Oh my God," said Corrie.

David said softly, "I guess we just found out what we were looking for."

Sebastian walked slowly across the room. He knelt down by the body and looked into its face.

"It's Danny Siddons," he said.

10

"IS HE DEAD?" Corrie asked.

Sebastian touched his arm, and Danny woke with a start. "What are *you* doing here?" he asked.

Sebastian said, "As Flinch would put it, 'I might ask you the same thing.' "

"We thought you were dead," David said.

"I knew he wasn't dead," Sebastian said, standing. "After all, corpses may swing from ropes, but they don't make ropes swing."

David and Corrie glanced at the rope. It had stopped moving.

"Were you sleeping, Danny?" David asked. He stepped forward. Corrie stayed back.

"I guess I dozed off," Danny said, rubbing his head. There was a large sweat stain on the front of his Siddons College T-shirt. "Got hot in here."

"Why *are* you here anyway?" Sebastian asked.

"I just . . . needed to get my head together. A place to think. Quiet. You know?"

Sebastian nodded. He understood the need to be alone and think things over. And he'd heard that

Danny hadn't been doing very well in college this past year.

"School trouble?" he asked.

"Nah. More like . . . girl . . . trouble."

"You've got a girlfriend?"

"I've got a girl," said Danny. "You surprised?"

"Why should I be surprised? You're old enough."

"Old enough to have a girl," Danny said with a sad laugh, "and old enough to have girl trouble."

"Oh, speaking of girls," Sebastian said, "this is Corrie Wingate. Her dad's the new minister."

Corrie didn't move. "Hi," she said.

"Hi, yourself," said Danny Siddons. "So you're taking over where Eric left off, huh?"

"What do you mean?"

"Oh, you know, minister's kid and all that."

Corrie smiled hesitantly. "Well, I'm a minister's kid. I'm not sure about 'all that.'"

"Aren't all minister's kids hell-raisers? Eric sure was. You look like you could be too."

Corrie wasn't sure whether to be insulted or complimented.

"Anyway," Danny went on, "you'll probably get into your share of trouble just hanging around with these two."

"It was usually Eric's fault we got into trouble," said David.

[36]

Sebastian said, "Danny, was Eric in trouble before he moved?"

"How should I know?"

"Maybe he said something."

Danny closed his eyes. Time hung heavy in the still, hot air. He said, "I don't think he mentioned anything. I don't think he was in trouble. But I'm not sure I remember."

He opened his eyes and mumbled something.

"What?" said Sebastian.

"I said I'm getting old," Danny replied. There was no humor in it.

"You're nineteen," Sebastian said.

"Doesn't that seem old to you? It sure does to me." Sweat dripped from the end of Danny's nose. He didn't notice. Or, if he did, he didn't care. Then he said, "I'll tell you one thing about your friend Eric."

"Danny!"

Ricky Siddons was standing at the top of the stairs.

"Hey, kid," said his older brother. "How's it going?"

Ricky had that old-peach look on his face again. Only this time it wasn't from concentration, it was from worry. He didn't say anything at first. Then, he said, "Come on, Danny. Let's go."

"Where we going?"

"Home," said Ricky.

Danny closed his eyes. No one moved. The room was stifling.

"We've got to go too," said Sebastian. "We'll see you, Danny."

Danny waved a hand in the air.

As they were about to descend the stairs, Sebastian turned and said, "Danny, you were going to say something about Eric."

Danny opened his eyes. "Was I?" He shook his head. "The mind's going, kid. And all because of a girl."

"Well, there's one thing I learned up there," Corrie said outside. "If the others are anything like those two, the Siddons family is very weird."

"Did you notice how Ricky shouted Danny's name?" David said. "I wonder how long he'd been standing there, anyway."

"I wonder what Danny was going to say about Eric," Corrie said.

Sebastian seemed lost in thought. "I don't know," he said absently.

"And what did Eric's note mean?" said David. "We didn't even have a chance to look around. Do you think maybe something's hidden up there?"

"We'll go back and check it out," Sebastian said.

"We can't this afternoon," said David. "We've got to go to the station."

"And I'm going to Hartford with my mom,"

said Corrie. "There's going to be a demonstration at City Hall. I was going to ask you guys if you wanted to go."

"We can't," said David. "Besides, we're not into that political stuff. Right, Sebastian?"

Sebastian didn't answer. He was watching Corrie's face change color.

"That's really dumb," she said. "If you live in the world, you've got a responsibility to be 'into that political stuff.' "

David shrugged. "If you say so," he said. "What do you think, Sebastian?"

"I think we'll have to wait until tomorrow morning to go back up into the tower. And maybe the next time there's a demonstration, we'll go with you, Corrie. Okay?"

Corrie tried to smile. But it wasn't easy.

"By the way," Sebastian said, "if you're home at seven tonight, turn on your radio."

"Why?" Corrie asked.

"You'll see," said Sebastian. He smiled at her.

Corrie smiled back. She wasn't sure why she was smiling. But this time it was easier.

11

"DO YOU THINK there's something wrong with us that we don't have girlfriends?" David said.

"What makes you ask?" Sebastian popped open the can of Mountain Dew, lifted it to his lips, and wished that just once he could drink soda without feeling guilty about it. That was his mother's fault.

"I don't know," David replied. "It seems like everybody's interested in girls all of a sudden. Ricky's got a girlfriend. And now Danny says he's got one. Even if she is making him miserable."

"Danny's nineteen," Sebastian said.

Soda in hand, David joined Sebastian on the cracked plastic furniture of WEB's reception area.

"But Ricky's our age," said David.

"*My* age," Sebastian corrected.

"Thirteen, twelve. What's the difference?"

"Maybe nothing," said Sebastian. "Maybe a lot."

"Why? You're not interested in girls, are you?"

Sebastian smiled.

"I hate it when you do that."

"Do what?"

"Smile like that. Mister Enigmatic."

"Big word for a twelve-year-old," Sebastian said.

"It's from my dad's new book—*The Case of the Enigmatic Fortune Cookie*. Anyway, you're changing the subject. I asked you if you're interested in girls."

Sebastian shrugged. "I don't see them as the enemy or anything. The way I look at it, girls are the same as boys, only different."

"May I quote you on that?"

Sebastian and David looked up. Will Barth was standing by the soda machine.

"Sure, Dad," said Sebastian. "You can quote me anytime."

"How'd the taping go today?" Will asked. He dropped some coins into the machine and said, "Don't tell your mother I'm drinking this junk."

"It went okay, Uncle Will," said David. "There have been finer hours in the history of broadcasting, but there have been worse."

"What was the show about?"

"Computer games," Sebastian said. "We had this kid from our school, Milo Groot, talk about this game he invented, and how 'you too can program your own games for fun and profit.'"

"Milo's a little demented," said David. "And he talks like this." He pinched his nose and said, " 'Well, Sebastian, that's an interesting question. I hope my answer won't be beyond the grasp of your listeners.'

[41]

And then he starts spouting all this technical stuff just to show you what a brain he is."

"Yeah, but it *was* pretty interesting," said Sebastian.

"Glad you understood it," David muttered.

Will Barth walked over to the sofa and asked his son kindly to remove his feet from where he wanted to sit. "You wouldn't put your feet all over the furniture at home," he said.

"This couch doesn't exactly command respect," Sebastian said.

"Got an idea for next week's show?"

"Not yet. But you know what I always say. Keep your eyes and ears open, and the idea will find *you*."

Will sighed and shook his head. "You sound like your mother."

"That's funny. She says I sound like you."

"David," Will went on, "I don't know how you let him get away with it. You're the writer for the show, after all."

Before David could reply, Harry Dobbs entered the room, a Braddock sister on each arm.

"Ah, Sebastian," he said. "Excellent show today. I heard a bit of the taping just now. Say, that Milo Groot's an impressive fellow, isn't he?"

David groaned.

"By the way, the girls here have a program idea for you."

The Braddock sisters giggled at being called girls, as well they might. Etta or Winnie (Sebastian could never remember which was which) said to Sebastian then, "We were just discussing it on our way over here today. We think it's something that should be brought to the public's attention."

"Yes," said the other (Winnie or Etta). "It's about time people heard *good* news about young people. If you believed everything you hear on the TV and the radio—oh, I mean no offense, Mr. Barth, but it's *true*, you know—you'd think the youth of today were nothing but worthless hooligans. But we know of a young man who is just the most wonderful, selfless—"

"He's part of a society at the college that visits shut-ins," said the first. "He comes to see Jeremy once a week, regular as the nine o'clock bell. You know about our cousin Jeremy, I'm sure. A young man, he's only in his sixties. But since the accident, he's had to live with us. Confined to a wheelchair, the poor thing. And so bitter he is. So bitter. Why, we thought he was a lost cause until this young man began to visit. Now he has something to look forward to every week. They play chess together, they talk. Sometimes Danny even reads to him—"

"Danny?" said Sebastian, sitting up. "Danny who?"

"Why, Danny Siddons. Well, of course, one expects only the best of the Siddons family, but I must say that Danny seems to outshine them all. Jeremy fairly dotes on him."

"Well," said Will Barth, "it sounds as if you might have a show there, Sebastian. Maybe you could even go to the Braddock house and interview Cousin Jeremy and Danny Siddons together."

Etta and Winnie Braddock clasped their hands to their respective bosoms. "What a glorious idea," said one.

"This will make a new man of Jeremy," said the other. "I can't wait to see his face when we tell him."

"Get serious," David said to Sebastian later when they were alone. "A show about a shut-in society? That's really boring, Sebastian."

"I have a hunch—" Sebastian started to say.

"I should have known."

"Always follow a lead. And keep your eyes and ears open."

"Yeah, yeah," David said. "And your hunch?"

"What about it?"

"What's your hunch?"

Sebastian smiled.

"Mister Enigmatic," said David. "And I still don't know if you're interested in girls."

12 "HELLO AGAIN. I'm Sebastian Barth, and this is 'Small Talk.' On to-night's show we're talking about electronic games. If you own a computer, you could be using it for more than *playing* games, you know. You could be *creating* games . . . and making money at the same time. That's what our guest did. Milo Groot is a student at Pembroke Middle School who . . ."

"I can't believe it!" Corrie cried. "Mom! Mom!"

Ginny Wingate stuck her head in her daughter's room. "What's all the yelling about?" she asked.

"My friend Sebastian has his own radio show," Corrie said. "I can't believe it. I've got to call him right now."

"You never told me," she said to Sebastian on the phone. Her words practically tripped over each other, they were in such a hurry getting out. "All that time we spent at the station yesterday, you didn't say a word. I've never known anybody who was famous. I mean, you're famous, right? You must be if you have your own show. I can't believe you didn't tell me. It just shows you don't know about people. Not even people you think you know."

[45]

When at last she managed to catch her breath, Sebastian said, "What are you doing talking to me instead of listening to the show?"

"Oh, right, right," said Corrie. "I'll call you back."

Later that night, Corrie had trouble falling asleep. The excitement of the demonstration that afternoon had been only a prelude to the excitement of her discovery about Sebastian. She was beginning to like it in Pembroke. Maybe the move hadn't been such a bad idea after all.

When at last she closed her eyes, she heard sounds outside her window. Rustling leaves. Snapping twigs. Whispers.

She went to the window and looked down. Someone was out there.

13

CORRIE KEPT shaking her head.

"I don't know," she said. "I don't know. It may have been Susan Siddons. Or maybe it was just somebody wandering around."

"Nobody wanders around a cemetery at night," Sebastian said. "Whoever it was was there for a reason."

David said, "It could have been some of the older kids hanging out."

"It was only one person."

"Besides," Sebastian said, "they all hang out on the green."

"I wish I'd been able to see better, but it was so dark last night."

"*I* wish I knew what we were looking for," David said. "Are we investigating a ghost? Are we searching for buried treasure? What are we doing up here anyway?"

The three friends had spent a good part of the morning exploring the bell tower, hoping to uncover something, anything, that would reveal to them the meaning of Eric's cryptic messages. So far, they had found nothing. As they rested, David noticed the faraway look in Sebastian's eyes. He knew that look well. It meant that Sebastian was thinking and, in all likelihood, would not share his thoughts until he was ready. As close as David felt to Sebastian, there was a part of his best friend that was off-limits even to him, a piece that belonged only to Sebastian Barth.

David's fingers played in a crack in the floor.

"Hey," he cried, "I found something."

Corrie and Sebastian looked at him as he picked at the crack.

"Look," he said, holding up his find. "Money." The single bill was tightly curled. David opened it and said, "A dollar. Oh, well, at least the morning hasn't been a total loss."

"Can I see that?" Sebastian asked.

David clutched the bill. "Finders keepers," he said.

"Don't be a baby. I'll give it back to you. I just want to see if there's anything special about it. Maybe that's what Eric wanted us to find."

After studying it, Sebastian shrugged and handed the bill back to David. "Looks pretty ordinary to me," he said.

"Maybe it's Danny's," said Corrie.

Pocketing the bill, David repeated, "Finders keepers."

And Sebastian's eyes got that faraway look.

14

THAT AFTERNOON, a third un-
signed letter arrived from Eric. This
one was typed. It read:

Squeak, squeak, the stairs do creak.
Beneath the third one take a peek.

15 SEBASTIAN GAVE it one last try, then put the hammer down.

"It's no use," he said. "It won't budge."

"We've tried the third step from the top," said David, "and the third step from the bottom. Maybe he didn't mean these stairs."

Sebastian wiped the sweat from his forehead. "He *must* have meant these stairs. First there was the note about the tower, then this one. They've got to connect."

"Unless he's pulling our leg," David said.

Sebastian nodded. "Unless he's pulling our leg."

Corrie had been studying Eric's note. "I have a hunch," she said.

"That's Sebastian's line," David protested. But Corrie paid no attention.

"Get off the stairs, you guys. Follow me."

Corrie descended the tower staircase and stood at the bottom. The boys did likewise.

"All right," she said. "I'm going to walk up the stairs. Listen for creaking. When you hear it, call it out."

Slowly, she began to climb the stairs. As her foot fell on each of the first three steps, there was only the sound of rubber touching wood, which is hardly a sound at all. The fourth step groaned.

"That's one," called David.

Fifth step, sixth step, not a sound. On the seventh step, there was a loud creaking noise.

"Two," said Sebastian and David together.

Corrie's foot on the eighth step produced a sound that was more a whisper than a creak. She looked back at the boys.

"Keep going," said Sebastian.

On the ninth step, there was nothing. On the tenth, there was a high-pitched squeal.

"Three," the three said together. And Corrie said, " 'Squeak, squeak, the stairs do creak. Beneath the third one take a peek.' He meant the third *creaking* stair, not just the third stair. This is it!"

Sebastian and David ran up the steps, two at a time. The lip of the third stair gave way easily to the hammer's prying. A flashlight revealed a surprisingly clean interior. And a simple gold ring.

Sebastian held it up to the light. In the curve of the band were engraved the initials, S.I.S.

16

"I CAN'T believe it," said Corrie. "It's her ring."

"It is hard to believe," Sebastian agreed.

"Do you think Eric knew it was here?" David asked. "Maybe he'd been looking for it, and the ghost followed him, and when he found it she pushed him down the stairs." He shook his head. "Listen to me. Talking about the ghost as if it's real. Your grandmother was right, Sebastian, all the talk about ghosts —or apparitions, or whatever you want to call them— is nothing but speculation. Nobody knows if there are *really* ghosts. But it seems like it must be true. Corrie's seen her twice—or at least once that we know of. And now this."

Sebastian turned the ring over in his hand. "Listen," he said, "if we want to find out the truth about this ghost, we've got some work to do. And we're going to have to split up to do it. David, I want you to go over to the historical society. There's a pretty good chance Gram will be there. Even if she isn't, find out everything you can about Susan Siddons. And Cornelius. And the ring. Oh, and while you're at it, see what you can learn about the legend of the First Church bell. Why is it rung every night at nine?"

"What are you going to do?" David asked, feeling his back pocket to make sure his notebook was there.

"I'm taking Corrie to meet somebody."

David frowned. "I could go with you," he said. "Corrie could go to the historical society."

"We have to use our strengths," said Sebastian, taking a tissue from his pocket to wrap the ring in. "You've got the head for books and facts and that sort of thing. And I need Corrie because she's new here. I'll explain everything later."

"But—"

"Meet us at the restaurant at three fifteen. That should give you plenty of time."

"Where are you going?"

"I'm going to find out who wrote that note."

"What do you mean? Didn't Eric—"

But Sebastian was already down the stairs and out of sight. Corrie hurried to follow after, turning back briefly at the bottom of the staircase. She looked at David with an expression that was part confusion, part sympathy.

A corner of David's mouth went up as he shrugged and said, "Mister Enigmatic."

17

"AH, BARTH, I listened to the show last night. And I must say, with all due modesty, that I found it one of your better programs."

With his large, aviator-frame glasses, bulbous head, and spiky hair, Milo Groot looked something like an intelligent scrub brush. In the fall, like Sebastian and Corrie, he would be entering the eighth grade. There was a difference, however. Milo was only ten.

"I'm glad you liked it," Sebastian said. "In fact, that's why I came to see you."

"For my advice on how to maintain such a high level of programming?"

"Not exactly. I'm thinking of doing a show about kids' writing. Since you're the editor of the school paper, I thought maybe you'd be a guest again. But I'd also like somebody who writes a lot."

"What about your friend Lepinsky? Doesn't he write for the program?"

"Yes, but that's just the reason I can't have him as a guest. No, I was thinking of whoever it is who writes those poems for the paper. You know, the ones that are signed 'Anony-Ms.' "

Milo Groot nodded. "Ah, yes," he said, picking his nose. Milo was in the habit of picking his nose when he thought. "But there is the question of ethics, Barth. Anony-Ms has chosen to use a pen name and, as her editor, I am unclear as to my ethical position in revealing her true identity."

Corrie watched Sebastian hold out two quarters. "Would this help clear matters up?" he asked.

"Janis Tupper," said Milo Groot, taking the money.

"Milo," a voice called from inside the house.

"I have to go," said Milo. "I'm helping my brother with his law boards. Let me know if I can be of further assistance, Barth. And don't tell Janis where you got her name."

"So much for ethics," said Sebastian, as Milo Groot's front door slammed shut.

Corrie and Sebastian were walking down Grandview Avenue.

"So you think Janis Tupper wrote that last note," Corrie said.

Sebastian nodded. "Eric couldn't write like that to save his life," he said. "Besides, it was written in the style of those poems in the school paper, the ones written by Anony-Ms, also known as Janis Tupper, also known as . . ."

Sebastian waved. A girl doing sit-ups on a lawn waved back.

"Also known as?" asked Corrie.

"Ricky Siddons's girlfriend." Sebastian pulled Corrie aside and said, "I've got to make sure Ricky stays out of my way tonight. And I need your help. Here's what I want you to do."

"THAT MILO GROOT! Did he tell you I was Anony-Ms?"

"Oh, come on. You didn't think it was a secret, did you? Everybody knows you're Anony-Ms. That's all everybody was talking about in school last year."

"Really?"

"Uh-huh. Anyway, if you've got some other poems or stuff you've written, I'd really like to look at them. Maybe you could read some of them on the air."

"On the radio? My poetry? Hey, that would be neat. Listen, I'll go get some right now. Wait here. I'll be back in a minute."

Ten minutes later, Janis Tupper reappeared with a stack of papers. She dumped them into Sebastian's arms.

"By the way," Sebastian said, as he and Corrie turned to leave, "have you seen that new movie yet?"

Janis shook her head. "We're going to the seven-o'clock show tonight. Have you seen it?"

"Yeah," said Sebastian. "It's really good. Ricky going with you?"

"Of course," said Janis.

"I haven't seen it," Corrie said. "It was coming to Troy just when we moved. I'd really like to."

"You want to come with us? A whole bunch of us are going tonight. You could meet everybody."

"That would be great."

"Come over about quarter to seven," said Janis, going into her sit-up routine again. "We can walk over to the theater together."

"Quarter to seven," Corrie said.

"Janis," said Sebastian, "what's all the exercise for? It's eighty-eight degrees."

"I'm getting in shape. There are cheerleader tryouts in August. You going to go out for cheerleader, Corrie?"

"Actually," said Corrie. "I was thinking of going out for the team."

"PERFECT," said Sebastian, as they rounded the corner of Janis's block. "Ricky will be out of the way tonight, and you'll be there to make sure he stays out of the way."

"What are you going to be doing?"

"I'm going to have a little talk with his brother Danny."

"And what are you going to do with all these poems?"

Sebastian looked down at the mass of papers in his arms. "I think she gave me everything she's written since Bert and Ernie taught her the alphabet. All I needed was one sample."

He sat down on the curb and removed a type-written poem from the top of the stack, then pulled Eric's latest letter from his pocket. He unfolded the letter and held the two side by side.

"Look," he said. "Every time the letter *t* appears in both the letter and the poem, it's a little below the line."

"Hey, you're right."

"It's definitely the same typewriter. There's no question about it—Janis Tupper wrote this note."

"But why?"

"That's just one more thing for us to find out."

The two fell silent. Leafy trees lined the street, providing some relief from the day's heat. Once in a while, a breeze stirred the leaves. Their rustling and the buzz and muted clang of construction somewhere else in town were the only sounds to be heard.

"It's really beautiful here," Corrie said. "I wasn't sure I was going to like Connecticut when I heard we were moving. I thought it would be a lot of cows or something."

"Come on," Sebastian said. "We're not meeting David for a couple of hours yet. And there really isn't anything for us to do right now. Let's drop this stuff off at my house, and I'll show you around Pembroke. There's a lot you haven't seen."

"Okay."

As they walked toward his house, Sebastian asked, "Were you serious about going out for the football team?"

"Sure," Corrie said. "Why shouldn't girls play football?"

"My mom's going to like you," said Sebastian.

18

HARVEST HOME

Here the Earth's Bounty Is Brought Home
from the Harvest
Let the Body Be Strengthened
And the Spirit Refreshed

Katie Hallem, Proprietor

"KATIE HALLEM," said Corrie. "That's your mother?" Sebastian nodded.

"How come her last name's different from yours?"

"She kept her own name when she married my dad."

"Oh," Corrie said. "And she has her own restaurant. That's neat. What kind of restaurant is it?"

"Natural foods," said Sebastian, as he pushed

open the door.

Inside, a ceiling fan whirred softly, stirring the hot air from its lethargy. Sitting at the table, drinking something yellow, was David Lepinsky. Across from him, with her back to the door, a woman was wiping her hands on her apron. When she heard the door open, she turned and said hello to her son.

Sebastian introduced Corrie.

Katie said, "If you two want something to drink, David's having a banana cooler. I, meanwhile, am having a nervous breakdown." It was hard to imagine Katie Hallem having a nervous twitch, let alone a breakdown. Looking at her, Corrie understood where Sebastian got his cool, calm demeanor.

"What's the matter, Mom?"

"There are mice in the rice," said Katie.

The kids laughed.

"It's not funny," Katie said. "I had to throw out a whole bag. And now I've got to go out and get more if I want to open for dinner. So if you'll excuse me...."

"Go ahead," said Sebastian. "We'll keep an eye on the place for you."

"You'll make Corrie a nice, cool drink?"

"Sure. I'll fix her up a tofu freeze. Sebastian grinned at Corrie.

Corrie grinned back. "I'll drink whatever you do," she said.

"In that case, we'll both have banana coolers."

As soon as Sebastian's mother had left, David

said, "Listen, I found out some really good stuff."

"Spill," said Sebastian.

"Well, first of all, there was this big scandal when Cornelius Siddons got married again."

"What do you mean, scandal?"

"Remember that Uncle Harry told us that Jenny—she's the woman Cornelius married—was a nurse. Well, the whole time Susan Siddons was sick, it was Jenny who took care of her. Your grandmother says that the family suspected there was something going on between Jenny and Cornelius even before Susan died. When they got married a year later, one of the daughters—Elvira, her name was—left town and never spoke to her father again. Now, before she left town, Elvira kept a diary—are you with me so far?"

Sebastian and Corrie nodded.

"The diary was written while she was living at home during the time her mother was sick. And she kind of dropped hints that something funny was going on between Cornelius and Jenny. She never came out and said so, *but*—there's one page missing from the diary. And your grandmother thinks that on that page she came right out and told what was going on. Probably the page was ripped out by someone in the family to protect the Siddons name."

"And Gram said the Siddonses didn't have any skeletons in their closet," Sebastian mused.

"Now, the thing about the bells is this. When Susan died, Cornelius bought the bell for First

Church and started ringing it in her memory every night at nine o'clock—that's the time she died. Then, when *he* died in 1923—and the weird thing is, he died at nine o'clock, too—the family began the tradition of ringing the bell twice. Once for her, once for him. Since then, one Siddons or another has rung the bell at nine every night. Your grandma says that until a few months ago, Danny's father did it. But then he had a heart attack. So Danny's been ringing the bell since. And, sometimes, he rings it more than twice. You know how upset your grandmother gets when that happens. She says it 'just isn't right.' "

Noisily, Sebastian sucked the last of his banana cooler up through his straw. "What else?" he asked David.

"Not much. I wasn't sure what I was looking for. I still don't know what you want all this for."

"To catch a ghost, you have to know more than the legend. You have to know the person behind it."

"Oh, there is something else," David said, "though it's no big deal. Your grandma got real excited about this because she just unearthed it, helping me with my research. It seems that Susan Siddons's middle name wasn't really Iris. It was Ivy. It was in some long-lost church record or something that she found that out. Seems Susan never liked the name Ivy, so she changed it."

"Is that it?"

"Yeah. Like I said, no big deal. Oh, there was

[63]

one other thing. And I've been saving this for last. There was a book at the historical society that had a lot of this stuff in it. It's called *Legends of Connecticut* or something like that. Anyway, three guesses who was the last person to take it out."

"I only need one," said Sebastian. Corrie watched him exchange a knowing look with David.

"Eric Mather," the two boys said together.

"Wait a minute," said Sebastian. "There's a phone call I need to make. I have this hunch. . . ."

It was Corrie's and David's turn to exchange looks.

"Well, hello there, Sebastian," said the voice on the other end of the phone. "To what do I owe the honor of this call?"

"Uncle Harry," Sebastian said, "remember when I asked you about the ghost the other day?"

"Yes?"

"You said someone else had asked you about Susan Siddons recently. Who was it?"

"Well, now," said Harry Dobbs, "I'm surprised he didn't mention it to you, seeing as how he was such a good friend of yours. It was the Mather boy. You know who I mean. Young Eric."

Sebastian reached into his pocket and pulled out a bit of tissue paper. He opened it and regarded the ring inside.

"Thanks, Uncle Harry," he said. "That's just what I needed to know."

[64]

19

IT WAS EVENING. A sudden down-
pour late in the day had caused more
than one Pembroke resident to echo the
sentiments of Mark Twain, who, it is said, remarked
of New England's weather: "If you don't like it, wait
a minute." All at once, the oppressive heat was gone.

Sebastian wondered if the change in the weather
was responsible for the change in Danny Siddons.

"Hey, guys," the bell ringer called out cheerily
as Sebastian and David appeared at the top of the
church-tower steps. "What's happening?"

"Not a whole lot," said Sebastian. "We were just
hanging around, nothing to do, you know. Thought
we'd come up and watch you do your thing."

"Do my *ring*, you mean!" Danny said.

"You're in a good mood."

"Hey, why not? You're only young once, right?"

"No more girl troubles?"

Danny looked surprised. "What are you talking
about?"

"Yesterday you said you were having a problem
with your girlfriend."

"Oh, that. Well, yesterday was yesterday, and

[65]

today is today. And today, I've got no-o-o problems. Hey, Sebastian, that girl is the best thing that ever happened to me. I'm serious, man. Makes me feel better than . . . than . . . anybody or anything ever has in my whole life."

"Sounds pretty good," said Sebastian.

"Is he talking about *girls?*" David whispered to Sebastian.

"Danny," Sebastian said, sliding to a sitting position against the wall, "you were going to tell us something about Eric yesterday. Do you remember what it was?"

Danny thought for a moment, then shrugged. "Beats me. The truth is, Sebastian, I was feeling so down yesterday I don't remember a lot of what I said. Nothing incriminating, I hope. Oops, time out."

Danny reached for the rope, one hand above the other, and pulled vigorously. The bell rang out from above. Again, he pulled. Again, the bell sounded. He looked at Sebastian and David looking at him and pulled the bell rope a third time.

"You did that the other night," Sebastian called out over the clamor. "You rang the bell four times. And tonight you rang it three times. What gives, Danny? I thought you were only supposed to ring it twice."

"It's for my girl," Danny said simply.

"Doesn't your family mind?" David asked. "I mean, it's sort of a family tradition to ring it only twice, isn't it?"

"Family tradition," Danny snorted. "Look, my family can say whatever they like. But it's me ringing the bell, isn't it? So I guess I can do it the way I want to do it. Instead of the Siddons way, I'm doing it the *Danny* Siddons way."

"But Cornelius—"

"Cornelius! The man died over half a century ago. Who cares anymore? I mean, around this town, everybody thinks the man was a saint. And if you're born a Siddons, it's instant sainthood for you too, buddy, like it or not. And you spend the rest of your life trying to deserve it. Or trying to convince people you do, anyway. Listen, the Siddons family may be big brass in this town, but don't forget—brass tarnishes."

Like the bell's reverberation, Danny's good mood had faded away. Nobody spoke again until Danny announced he was leaving.

"Meeting your girl?" Sebastian asked.

"Some of her friends," Danny replied softly. He picked up a green backpack and strapped it on.

As they walked out into the night, Sebastian said, "Oh, by the way, I was thinking of doing a show about that shut-in society of yours."

"How'd you hear about that?" Danny said.

"The Braddock sisters. They told me—"

"They told you I've been visiting old Jeremy, huh?"

"Yeah. They thought it would be a good idea to interview the two of you. Talk about the shut-in society, you know. Improve the image of American youth. The Braddock ladies think you're really something special."

"Well, forget it," said Danny Siddons, as Sebastian's cool, green-gold eyes studied him. "I'm not something special. I'm just Danny. Siddons or not, I'm not a saint. And I don't want you making me into one, Sebastian. You understand? So just forget it."

Danny took off in a run.

"Boy," said David, "what's bugging him all of a sudden?"

"I don't know," Sebastian answered. "But I have a hunch how we can find out."

"How?"

"By following him. Come on."

20

DANNY WAS moving fast. His bouncing backpack gave Sebastian and David something to focus on as he raced down Main Street and across the village green into that part of town known as "the railroad district." Here, restored buildings full of charm and high prices rubbed shoulders with run-down bars and pool halls and a seedy hotel that had once been the town's pride. The train station across the street—defunct but preserved for show, like a corpse when the undertaker's through—gave the place its name. Now, the Terminal Hotel was a way station not for well-heeled travelers but for the down-and-out and the dispossessed, and its name had taken on a different significance entirely. The residents leaned out of their plastic-patched windows and watched life's slow parade pass them by.

This night, they saw a young man in a hurry followed by two furtive boys.

Danny disappeared down Water Street, an alley more than a street, which ran along the backs of several buildings and exuded the oily smell of danger. Sebastian and David peered around the corner of

Folsom's Bar & Grill. Water Street was dotted with several yellow light bulbs and a red one flickering on and off, and none of them spelled welcome. They heard the steady dripping of water into a pool that shimmered in the yellow light. They didn't hear footsteps. They didn't see Danny Siddons.

"What'll we do?" David whispered.

Sebastian put a finger to his lips, then motioned for David to follow.

They inched their way along the worn brick exterior of Folsom's. On the other side of the wall, muffled voices, thick with drink, poured secrets into strangers' ears. A sudden laugh. A cough. The plink, plink, plink of water falling into a shimmering pool. Sebastian and David hardly dared breathe as the sounds and the silence grew louder. The brick beneath their fingers perspired. In the distance, a shadow suddenly appeared, loomed large and fell away.

"It's him."

"He turned left, I think."

The boys picked up their pace, leaving Folsom's and the first circle of yellow light behind. They moved in darkness past several other buildings, emerging in light near the end of Water Street, running now toward the spot where they'd seen the shadow. Voices rushed to meet them from around a corner. They fell back against a sooty gray building and listened. They were breathing hard now. The smell of danger was stronger; its oiliness coated their nostrils.

They couldn't hear the words being spoken but they made out several voices: men's, boys', they didn't know how many.

"Get low," Sebastian whispered. He dropped to all fours and crept along the base of the building, dusting himself with soot. David followed.

When Sebastian reached the corner, he poked his head out and looked into the sullen darkness of the alley's ell. Fifty-or-so feet away, inside what looked like an old warehouse, Danny Siddons paced back and forth. The single bulb over his head shed a white light on the small crowd gathered around him. Sebastian didn't recognize any of the faces, or the voices that went with them. He turned to tell David he was going to move in closer. It was then that he saw the figure standing in the yellow pool of light next to Folsom's Bar & Grill.

"Move back," Sebastian commanded, almost forgetting to keep his voice down.

"Where?"

"Back up. There's a doorway. Hurry."

The boys moved quickly along the wall until they found the doorway and pressed themselves into its shadows.

A moment later, the figure approached, and they saw that it was Ricky Siddons. David cupped his hand over his mouth to keep from giggling, something he was apt to do when he was nervous. Ricky stopped just a few feet away from where they were huddled, turned, looked almost into their eyes, and walked on. David let out a sigh. In a moment, they heard a loud exchange of voices.

"What the hell are you doing here?"

"I'm not going to let you do it, Danny."

"This is none of your business, Rick. Now, get out of here and leave me alone."

"I'm going to tell, Danny. I don't want to, but I will if I have to."

There was the heavy thud of flesh hitting flesh. A curse. And the sounds of a scuffle.

"Stop it, Danny. Let go of me. Stop it."

There were other voices calling out to Danny to stop. He did, and then there was the sound of heavy breathing.

The other voices retreated. The only voice left belonged to Danny. "Just keep out of this, Ricky," he said. "Leave me alone, you hear what I'm telling you? Leave me alone."

It seemed to Sebastian and David that Danny and the others had gone back inside the warehouse. For a time, the only sound was the plink, plink, plink of water dripping. Then the two heard footsteps. Ricky Siddons walked by. They waited until they thought he'd reached the street before they peered out.

Ricky was slumped in the pool of yellow light against the wall of Folsom's Bar & Grill. His head was cradled in his arms. Soon there was another sound on Water Street. It was the sound of crying.

21

THE MOANING grew louder.

Corrie shivered as she entered the cemetery.

It had been half an hour since she'd arrived home from the movies. Her sister Alice had been on the phone, so she'd been unable to call Sebastian as she'd planned. She'd gone out to the back porch, and it was there that she'd heard it. A long, low moan. A woman's moan. It made her think of stories she'd heard of women whose husbands went out to sea and never returned. It was the moan of a woman who had lost someone she loved.

Her feet were gritty inside her sandals as she made her way slowly through the darkness, bumping against toppled tombstones, stubbing her bare toes on rocks. The air was cool now, dry and motionless. She felt its dryness in her throat, or was it the dryness of fear?

The moaning became a sort of sobbing, and Corrie stopped. It was coming from several feet away. There wasn't enough light to make out the lettering on the stone, but Corrie knew well enough that she was standing before Susan Siddons's grave. She stood, transfixed, and gazed into the darkness as if she were watching the sound. She didn't know what else to do. Even if she hadn't been afraid, she wouldn't have needed to look behind the stone. There was no doubt in her mind. The mournful sounds were coming from *within* the grave.

Her shivering grew worse.

Suddenly, a wisp of smoke rose from the grave. Corrie closed her eyes, then opened them, to be sure they were not playing tricks on her. The smoke continued to rise. The sobbing became a moan again and and the moan grew louder as the smoke rose higher. Corrie felt her arms grow prickly. She shuddered as a chill whispered along the back of her neck.

All at once, the moaning stopped. The smoke vanished. A voice said, "You have my ring." Standing fifty feet in front of her was a figure in black. The figure raised its white-gloved hand. And Corrie turned to run.

22

SHE RAN without seeing. A cold sweat clung to her forehead. She stumbled through the cemetery gate and fell into someone's arms. A scream stayed stuck in her throat.

"Corrie," he said, "what's wrong?"

Corrie tried to catch her breath. "Oh, Sebastian. I...I..."

"Calm down. Gee, you look really pale."

"Yeah," said David, "like you've seen a ghost or something."

"Very funny," Corrie said. She was trembling.

Sebastian, suddenly aware of his hands on Corrie's arms, removed them and looked at her with concern.

"Was it her again? Did you see Susan Siddons?"

"More than that. I think I'm going crazy. I really do." She told them all that she had seen and heard. David looked at her skeptically; Sebastian didn't appear to doubt a word she was saying.

"Let's take a look," he said when she had finished.

"I'm not going back in there."

"All right, we'll go. Do you have a flashlight?"

Corrie nodded, and the boys followed her into the house. A few minutes later, Sebastian and David made their way toward Susan Siddons's grave.

"Smoke rising out of the grave!" David muttered. "Moans! I think she's right, Sebastian—she *is* going crazy."

Sebastian didn't say a word as he passed over the sanctified ground. The flashlight's beam revealed nothing more than earth and grass, rocks and gravestones. There was no sign of smoke or any indication that Susan Siddons had been there in flesh or spirit. Her grave seemed undisturbed. Sebastian led David to the bushes near the back fence of the cemetery. There was nothing there.

"You see what I mean?" said David. "She didn't hear or see anything. She's just being hysterical."

"Corrie isn't the type to get hysterical," Sebastian said. "I'm pretty sure she saw and heard everything she said she did."

"But—"

Sebastian was gone before David could finish his sentence.

"We didn't see anything," he told Corrie back outside the gate, "but that doesn't prove a thing. After all, if it was really the ghost, she wouldn't have left any traces, would she?"

Corrie shook her head weakly. "I want to go in," she said.

[77]

"We have a lot to talk about," said Sebastian. "Let's all meet at my house in the morning."

"Good night," Corrie said.

"Good night."

Sebastian turned off the flashlight and handed it to her.

The boys stood in the darkness without speaking. They heard Corrie's back door squeak open and shut. They listened to the crickets chirping. After a time, they turned to go. A cloud passed between them and the moon.

23

"FEELING BETTER?"

Corrie smiled as she came up the walk to Sebastian's house. Sebastian was waiting at the door.

"David's out back," he said.

A few minutes later, Sebastian was bouncing a basketball on the flagstone of the patio. "The thing of it is," he said, "I'm not so sure anymore that Eric's notes have anything to do with the ghost. I'm almost positive they're about Danny."

"But that doesn't make sense," said David.

"Let me finish," Sebastian said, catching the ball on the rebound and holding it, poised, between his hands. "Danny was going to tell us something about Eric when Ricky stopped him, remember? What if he was about to say, 'That friend of yours is too nosy for his own good.' Maybe Eric found out something about Danny that Danny didn't want him to know. And when he heard about it, Danny pushed Eric down the tower stairs as a warning."

"But that's just one little thing that Danny said . . . or didn't say," said Corrie. "What about my seeing the ghost? And what about the notes themselves?"

"I've been trying to rethink the notes," Sebastian replied. "The easiest is the one that said, 'In the tower.' That *could* mean Danny, right? I mean, Danny's in the tower every night at nine, and Eric and Ricky used to hang out there with him all the time. The one about the third step probably means just what we thought it did—look under the third squeaky step."

"But the ring . . ."

"Well, I have a theory about that too. It's a long shot, but here it is. What if Ricky somehow found out about Eric's notes? After all, his girlfriend wrote one of them, so he must have known about them. And what if Eric's notes were trying to tell us something about Danny . . . something serious, something dangerous, something Ricky knew too and wanted to be sure we didn't find out? So Ricky made it look like the notes had to do with the ghost. He may have planted that ring inside the stair and taken out whatever it was he didn't want us to find."

Sebastian bounced the ball to Corrie, who took it and gave it a twirl. She said, "Maybe we should take another look."

"Good idea."

As they walked down Chestnut Street, Sebastian said, "I have a hunch that Ricky is the key."

"And the ghost?"

"Like I said, Ricky might be setting the whole thing up to throw us off the track."

"You don't think the ghost is real?"

"I'm not ruling that out. I'm just trying to think it through from another angle."

"You know," Corrie said, "Ricky was acting strange last night. After the movie, he and Janis had a big fight. I didn't hear it; they were walking ahead of everybody else. All of a sudden, he just took off. Janis was real upset."

"That must have been right before we saw him on Water Street," said David.

Sebastian told Corrie all that they had seen and overheard in the alley the night before. Then he asked, "Did Janis say anything about the fight afterwards?"

"Not at first. She just got quiet. Then she said she wanted to go home. I said I'd go with her, and while we were walking, she started to tell me all about it. She said Ricky's changed a lot recently. He's gotten moody and won't talk when she asks what's bothering him."

"Just like Eric," said David.

"Does Janis have any idea what's bugging him?"

"That's what they fought about. She told him she couldn't take his being so moody all the time. And he just ran off. The funny thing is, after she told me that, she stopped talking too. As if she knew more but wouldn't tell me."

"If only there were some way you could get her talking again," Sebastian said.

"I'm meeting her later today. We're going to the mall."

"Great. See what you can find out. And while you're at it, you could mention the weird notes I've been getting from Eric. Check out her reaction."

The kids entered First Church and climbed the stairs. After checking out the bell tower to be sure they were alone, they pried open the top of the third squeaky stair.

"Empty," said David.

Sebastian kept staring into it.

"You see something we don't?" David asked.

Sebastian shook his head. "There's nothing to see," he said. "No dust balls, no wood splinters. Nothing at all."

"So?"

"It just seems a little *too* clean, that's all." Sebastian replaced the top of the step and started down the stairs.

"I hate to say it, Sebastian," Corrie said, "but, clean or not, an empty stair does put a hole in your theory."

"Yeah," David said. "Not only that, but what about the *first* note? The one that read 'S.I.S.'?"

"Oh, I've thought about that one plenty," said Sebastian, with that faraway look in his eyes.

"And?"

"And S.I.S. doesn't have to stand for Susan Iris Siddons, you know."

"Whose initials are they, then?"

"They don't have to be anybody's initials. It may just be a coincidence, but think about it: what are the first three letters of the words *shut-in society?*"

24

"I DON'T KNOW what you're talking about, I'm sure," said the woman behind the desk. Her hair, a mountain of shiny curlicues, looked like something you'd be afraid to touch in a gift shop.

"A shut-in society," Sebastian said. "For visiting people who can't get out. You know?"

"Well, I'm not saying it isn't a good idea," the woman replied, sticking a pencil in a crack in her hair. "I'm just saying that I don't know of any such society here at Siddons College. But you may be in the wrong office."

Sebastian glanced over his shoulder at the sign on the door. "This is the Office of Student Activities," he said.

"That's right," said the woman. "But it could be an activity of one of the fraternities. And then we wouldn't know about it."

"This person," David said, "doesn't belong to a fraternity."

"Well, I tell you what." She twisted the pencil in her hair as if sharpening it. "You go over to the dean's office and ask for Gladys. She's Dean Ward's secretary. She knows *everything* that goes on on campus. If she doesn't know about this shut-in society of yours, believe me, it doesn't exist."

GLADYS KEPT shaking her head. "There's no shut-in society," she said firmly. "If I don't know about it—"

"It doesn't exist," said Sebastian. "Thank you."

"You're welcome. But what is it you boys want with a shut-in society?"

"My grandfather is confined to his bed," Sebastian said.

"Yeah," said David, "he needs someone to change the channels for him."

Gladys gave the boys a look. "Ever hear of remote control?"

Sebastian's face brightened. "Thank you, ma'am," he said.

"Now why didn't we think of that?" David asked.

Gladys sighed.

As the boys turned to leave, they caught a glimpse of a familiar figure inside Dean Ward's office. Police Chief Alex Theopoulos was a good friend of David's dad and a frequent visitor to the Lepinsky home. He was wearing his uniform, which meant he was on duty. Alex turned and saw the boys looking at him. He waved. They waved back.

"What's he doing here?" Sebastian asked.

"Just wait until you boys start college," said

Gladys. "You'll know then what a policeman is doing on a campus. If there are ninety-nine laws, a hundred of 'em will be broken by kids with nothing better to do. Rebels, that's what they are. Who says James Dean is dead?"

"Who's James Dean?" said Sebastian.

David, who was well read on the subject of ancient movie stars, was about to answer when Gladys said, "Then again, maybe he's on the lookout for boys who tell cockamamie stories about grandfathers who can't change their own channels. What is it you boys *really* want to know, anyway?"

"Good-bye," said Sebastian, grabbing David's arm and shoving him out the door.

"Good-bye," said Gladys.

25

"SO THERE'S no shut-in society," David said, as the boys pedaled their way back into town. "What's Danny doing visiting Jeremy Braddock, then?"

"That's what I'll try to find out when I interview them."

"You're still going to interview them for the show? But if there isn't a shut-in society—"

"Ah, but *they* say there is."

"But what if they won't let you talk to them? Remember how mad Danny got when you said you wanted to."

"You underestimate the power of the Braddock sisters," Sebastian said. "And the power of the press. Hey, look who's here."

Ricky Siddons coasted down his driveway and onto Parksdale Road. Bringing his shiny gold ten-speed to a sudden stop, he looked at Sebastian and David like a rabbit caught in the glare of oncoming headlights. He didn't seem to know which way to turn.

"Hey, Ricky," Sebastian called out. "Long time, no see. Whatcha been up to?"

"Nothin' much."

The two boys hit their brakes and straddled the bars of their bikes.

"How's Danny doing?" Sebastian asked.

Ricky rubbed his left biceps as if it were sore. "What do you mean?" he said.

"Well, he told us he was having girl trouble."

"Girl trouble?"

"Yeah," said David, "as in girlfriend, you know."

Ricky grunted. "Danny doesn't have any girlfriend. He'd probably be better off if he did."

"I don't get it," said Sebastian. He and David exchanged glances.

Ricky started to say something but didn't.

"Where you headed?" Sebastian asked him.

"Over to Janis's."

"She won't be home. She's out at the mall with Corrie."

"Oh. Well, then, I'll just go in and hang out on the green. See who's around."

"We'll ride with you," Sebastian said.

They didn't talk the rest of the way into town. When they got to the green, they saw a handful of boys attached to the bandstand like permanent fixtures.

"You guys coming?" Ricky said.

"I don't think so," said Sebastian. "By the way,

I'm going to do a story on your brother and Jeremy Braddock for my show."

Ricky shrugged. "So?"

Sebastian returned the shrug. "Nothing. Just wondering if you belong to that shut-in society of Danny's. If you do, I could put you on the show too."

Ricky almost laughed. "Danny has a shut-in society? That's a good one. Listen, I don't know anything about that. I do know he visits old man Braddock. Don't ask me why. I guess there's some good in Danny somewhere." He made this last statement more to himself than to the others.

"When did he visit Mr. Braddock last?" asked Sebastian. "Do you know?"

"Sure. Yesterday afternoon. Why?"

"No reason."

The boys on the bandstand were calling Ricky's name. But Ricky's attention was on Sebastian.

"Why are you asking all these questions about Danny?" he said.

"No reason. Does it make you nervous?"

Ricky's face blanched. Then he forced his lips into a stiff smile. "Of course not," he said. "Why should it? Just seems kind of strange, that's all."

"Life is full of strange things," said Sebastian, as he and David rode off.

"We sure are finding out a lot about Danny today," David said. "First there's no shut-in society.

Now there's no girlfriend. He said he was ringing the bell for his girl, Sebastian, remember? Why do you suppose he's lying?"

"Simple. The extra bells are a code. And last night we figured out what the code meant."

"We did?" David looked surprised.

"Didn't we?" said Sebastian. There was a smile in his green-gold eyes as he picked up speed and disappeared around a corner.

26 WHEN CORRIE returned from the mall, she found Sebastian and David in her front yard playing monkey-in-the-middle with Buster.

"Hey, Corrie," Buster cried out when he saw his sister, "I'm the monkey."

"Tell me something I don't already know," Corrie said.

"It's about time you got here," said David, tossing the ball to Buster.

"I got it!" Buster shrieked. "I'm not the monkey! I'm not the monkey!"

"Tell Mom the good news," said Corrie.

"Okay," Buster said. He ran into the house.

Corrie shook her head. "It's amazing. He always does what I tell him to. If only he'd stay five forever."

"I hate to change the subject...." said Sebastian.

"I wish I had something to tell you," Corrie replied, dropping down onto the front steps of the house, "but it was like Dr. Jekyll and Mr. Hyde with Janis today."

"What do you mean?"

"I mean, the way she acted, last night never happened. When I said something about Ricky and the fight, she just brushed me off as if there was nothing to talk about. And she calls Ricky moody!"

"Sounds to me like she didn't *want* to talk, not that there was nothing to talk about."

"Yeah, after awhile I figured that too."

David asked, "Did you mention Eric's notes?"

"Mm-hmm," Corrie said with a nod. "She looked a little surprised at first. Then she played dumb. 'Notes?' she said. 'What notes? I never heard about any notes.' I mean, it was pretty obvious she knew all about them. But she was too smart to admit it. And then she changed the subject."

"I guess we were luckier with Ricky today," David said.

Sebastian nodded. His gaze was fixed on the cemetery past the white fence surrounding Corrie's house.

"Let's pay a visit to Susan Siddons," he said. "Maybe we'll see something today we didn't see last night."

Moments later, Corrie said, "*There's* something I never noticed before. Or if I did, I guess I didn't really pay attention." She bent down and ran her hands over the worn gravestone. Her fingers traced the outline of vines and leaves that were engraved on it.

"I guess that's supposed to be the poison ivy," David said.

Corrie pulled her hand back and laughed. "Hope it isn't catching," she said. Then she read from the epitaph, " 'Tis a garden of poison'd ivy, And the roots lie here below.' " She thought for a minute. "I wonder," she said, "if the roots really do lie below."

Sebastian looked at her quizzically.

"I mean, does the engraving on the stone go below the dirt?" Without thinking, she picked at the earth at the stone's edge. To her surprise, it moved easily in her hands. "Hey, it's loose."

Sebastian and David knelt down beside her. "Not only that," said Sebastian, "but the grass here is a different color." He gave the grass a gentle tug, and a patch of it lifted off as easily as a cheap toupee.

"It's Astroturf or something like that," said David.

Sebastian ran his fingers through the exposed dirt. "It really is loose. Somebody's been messing around here."

"Grave robbers," said David.

"What do you think?" Corrie asked Sebastian.

"I don't know. But I have a hunch."

David stood up, and as Corrie and Sebastian continued to puzzle over their discovery, he began poking around for other clues. When he got to the bush at the back of the cemetery, he let out a yell. Sebastian and Corrie ran to him.

"I thought it was a snake," David said.

Under the bush, tucked away so that Sebastian and David had missed seeing it the night before, was a coiled length of rubber hose.

"It does look like a snake," Corrie said. "A sleeping one."

"Or one that's about to strike," Sebastian commented. And then he said, "Curiouser and curiouser."

27 THAT NIGHT, Sebastian stopped by the Lepinsky house and found David and his father absorbed in a game of chess. Their hands shushed him as he entered the front room. A fuzzy glow from a nearby floor lamp encircled the chessboard. The rest of the room was dark. In a corner, Sebastian made out Rachel Lepinsky sitting primly in a high-backed chair, a black sweater draped over her head and buttoned under her chin. Her hands were folded in her lap; her lips moved, but there was no sound coming through them.

Sebastian was wondering what to do with himself when he heard Josh say, "Checkmate." The game was over.

"You're getting better," said Josh. He ran his hand over his head and commented, "And I'm getting balder."

"Well, if there's any relationship between the two," David said, standing and stretching, "maybe I should wait until you've gone completely bald before I play you again."

"Over my dead body," Josh said, giving his son a swat on the behind.

"No thanks, I don't want to wait *that* long," said David.

"So, Mr. Barth," Josh said, "can I interest you in a game? Or are you here to spend time with someone nearer your own age with all his hair?"

"Josh," Sebastian said, "if I ever figure out what's supposed to be so interesting about chess, you'll be the first one I'll tell."

There was a knock on the door. "Anybody home?" came a hearty baritone.

"Holy Mother of Pearl," cried Josh. "It's the coppers."

Alex Theopoulos let himself in. Even out of uniform, he carried his authority as naturally as a mother cat carries her young. He was a big man, barrel-chested, with large, hairy arms built for power and affection. As police chief of Pembroke, he didn't always see the best that human nature had to offer, but he never stopped believing that the best was inside everyone, even the hardest criminal. "People are a little like nuts," he sometimes said. "Crack the toughest shell and you just may find the sweetest meat." Next to Sebastian's mom and dad, he was Josh Lepinsky's closest friend.

"I've got you covered," Alex said, pulling a bar of chocolate out of his pocket.

Josh stretched out his hand. "You shouldn't have," he said.

"I didn't. It's for Rachel. Where is she anyway?"

Josh nodded toward the corner.

"Huh?"

Josh shrugged, as if to say, "Don't ask."

"Well, when she comes out of her trance, give her this, will you?" He handed the bar to David. "And what were you boys doing over at the college today? Early enrollment?"

"No, Alex," David said. "We were just checking something out. What were *you* doing there?"

Alex dropped into a chair and switched on a lamp. "You in mourning here?" he said. "Now, what'd you ask me? Oh, yeah. What was I doing at Siddons? Just routine. I check in over there a couple of times a week to see what's going on. There's been a rash of vandalism the last few weeks...broken windows, that sort of thing. Some summer students working off a little steam, I guess. Other than that, a little petty thievery, drugs, term-paper scams...."

"What are you talking about?" Josh said. "Not *our* Siddons College. Not *my* students." Josh taught a course in creative writing.

"No, you're right," Alex said. "Your students probably aren't into drugs. You keep their minds clouded enough without them. But don't kid yourself, Josh. Pretty little Siddons College with its pretty little students has the same problems as every other campus in the country. Appearances can be deceiving."

"Now where did I hear that before?" Josh asked.

"You said it," said Sebastian. "To me. The other day."

"Did I? Imagine that. Listen, Alex, I need your help on something. Can you take a look at this chapter I just wrote? I'm not sure I've got the police procedure right."

"Sure, sure."

The two men left the room. David noticed that Sebastian was deep in thought.

"Sebastian?" he said after a moment.

Sebastian jerked his head in David's direction. "I've been thinking," he said.

"So I see."

"I need you to do some reading. Okay?"

"Sure. What about?"

"Let's go up to your room, and I'll tell you."

As the boys started to mount the stairs, Sebastian turned back and said, "Okay, Rachel, I give up. What are you supposed to be?"

Rachel lifted her head slowly. "I'm not supposed to *be* anything," she said. "I'm practicing."

"For?"

"I'm thinking of becoming a nun."

"Rachel, I hate to point this out," said Sebastian, "but you're Jewish."

Rachel thought for a moment, then said, "So call me a trend setter."

28

THE NEXT DAY was Saturday. Sebastian received a fourth note in the mail:

Before the fall, a flash of white.
After the fall, black as night.

29

ON SUNDAY, Sebastian accompanied his parents and grandmother to church. They were not regular churchgoers but, like so many others in town, felt it only proper to attend on Drew Wingate's first Sunday as minister. The sanctuary was nearly filled when they arrived; they squeezed into a back row and opened their hymnals to "Nearer, My God, To Thee," page 247. Sebastian managed to get out every fifth word or so as he scanned the room for familiar faces. In one of the boxed pews near the front, he spotted Corrie. On one side of her were her mother and sister; on the other were her two younger brothers. They were fighting, and Mrs. Wingate kept reaching behind Corrie's back and tapping the older one on the shoulder. It didn't seem to do much good.

In the choir, their mouths open angelically in song, were Danny and Ricky Siddons.

When the hymn was ended and the congregation seated, Drew Wingate stepped forward to speak. Except for some whispering in the fourth pew (Ginny Wingate telling her sons to be still or they could just leave this minute and humiliate the entire family), there wasn't a sound.

Drew Wingate stood for a moment beaming at the congregation. He looked like a big red-cheeked kid standing in a bakery with a dollar in his pocket. He was happy to be there, and his happiness permeated the room. His sons stopped their bickering. His wife withdrew her admonishing gaze and replaced it with a proud one, which she turned on her husband.

Someone coughed.

"I know this is not the customary place in our service for announcements," Drew Wingate said, "but I just want to extend a word of welcome. No, not to myself. You've all made me feel more than welcome by your presence this morning. I can only say I hope I'll feel this welcome *every* Sunday."

The congregation chuckled at the minister's little joke.

"No," he went on, "the word of welcome is not for me, but for someone as special to First Church as he and his family are to Pembroke. Travis Siddons is one of our hardest-working deacons and, until recently, a member of our choir. As you all know, Travis suffered a heart attack some months ago, and this is, I understand, his first Sunday out. Welcome back, Travis. We're glad you're here."

Travis Siddons stood and acknowledged Drew Wingate's words. He turned so that Sebastian caught sight of his face before he sat down again. Sebastian had never known Ricky's and Danny's father well; he had met him only once or twice. He knew that he was an important man, a busy man. He had heard it said repeatedly that he was a good man. But what he saw was a man with hard eyes and a hard mouth that even illness couldn't soften.

Sebastian looked to the choir loft. Danny stared at his father with contempt.

30

THAT AFTERNOON, Sebastian went over to the Lepinskys.

Rachel appeared at the door wearing an apron and stirring a bowl of cookie batter. With the black sweater draped over her head, she looked more like a nine-year-old Italian grandmother than a nun. Sebastian said, "Hey, Rachel, how's it going?" and bounded up the stairs to David's room.

"Peace be with you, my son," Rachel replied.

"So," said Sebastian, slamming the door behind him, "what did you find out?"

David was lying on his bed, reading an old copy of *Natural History*. He rolled over onto his side and looked up at Sebastian. "Barn owls, unlike bats, do not use sonar," he said.

"Thanks. I'll be sure to remember that the next time barn owls come up in conversation. You know what I mean—what did you find out from the reading I asked you to do?"

David reached for the notebook lying on his nightstand. He held it up. "Everything you wanted to know is right here," he said. "I didn't even have to go to the library. I just looked in some books my dad has. I found out some pretty interesting stuff, let me tell you."

"Can I borrow that?"

"Sure." David handed the notebook to Sebastian.

As Sebastian flipped through its pages, he asked, "Is everything in here, from the beginning?"

"You mean all that stuff about the ghost and the legends and all that?"

Sebastian nodded.

"It's in there. But what do you want it for?"

"Just putting the pieces together. Besides, I don't think we've heard the last of the ghost yet. I'll see you later."

"See you. Oh, wait, there's something I forgot to tell you."

"What's that?"

"The maximum binaural time difference for barn owls is about a hundred and fifty microseconds."

"I'll keep it in mind," Sebastian said.

THERE WAS a spot a couple of miles from the center of town where Sebastian often went to be alone. Down a dirt road off Route 7 were the ruins of an old stone house. Sebastian liked it here among the worn stones and the green trees and ivy. In all the times he'd come, he'd never seen another person. This place was his alone. He usually sat on a high-backed stone bench some distance from the house. He often wondered who had put the bench there, who had lived in the house, and what had become of them.

Today he wondered whether there had ever been a barn and, if so, if there'd been barn owls.

After an hour, he closed the notebook and stared at the vine-covered chimney. He was not really surprised at the facts David had put together, only that they confirmed his theory so neatly. There were only two things left to do, he thought. The first was to interview Danny Siddons and Jeremy Braddock.

When he got home, he called the Braddock sisters and was told by Etta or Winnie that Jeremy would be delighted to see him the next day. They would call Danny Siddons and be sure he was there as well. Their only question of Sebastian was what kind of cookies he liked. They'd make up a batch special.

Double chocolate chip, he told them.

31 "DOUBLE CHOCOLATE CHIP," said the Braddock sister in the pink dress. She handed the plate of cookies to Sebastian, who in turn passed it on to Corrie and David.

The other sister, wearing a blue dress that looked too warm for the time of year, said, "How nice that you brought your friends along. It's so seldom we have young people in our house. Except for Danny, of course."

"David writes for the show," said Sebastian. "He always comes with me on interviews. And Corrie is—"

"Oh, *we* know who Corrie is. Goodness, I should think so," said the pink sister. "Wasn't that a wonderful sermon Reverend Wingate preached yesterday, Etta?"

Etta (the blue sister) nodded. "We are very lucky to have Reverend Wingate as our minister, Corrie," she said. "And I'm sure you feel fortunate to have him as your father."

Corrie was never sure how to respond to that sort of statement. But she was well practiced in dealing with old people, especially the doting kind. She smiled politely and said, "Yes, ma'am. He's a wonderful person."

The two sisters nodded at each other.

"I don't know what's keeping Jeremy and Danny," said Etta.

Sebastian was surprised. "Is Danny here already?"

"Oh, yes," Winnie said. "He arrived about twenty minutes before you did. Jeremy insisted that he come to his room at once. He said he had some rare books to show him."

"We never knew he *had* any rare books," Etta confided. "He's not much of a reader, you know. Never has been. And not much of a collector, either. Says he can't abide the clutter of human existence."

A door opened somewhere in the house. The sound was followed by a steady, rhythmic squeaking.

Etta poured the kids more milk and shook her head. "I do wish he'd oil that wheelchair more often. We've offered to do it for him, but he wants none of it. Says he prefers it to squeak so he doesn't sneak up on himself unawares."

In a whisper, Winnie said, "Cousin Jeremy does say the most peculiar things sometimes."

Just then, a corpulent man in a bright Hawaiian shirt wheeled himself into the room. A fly buzzed around his head, attracted no doubt by the beads of sweat there. This was Cousin Jeremy. He was followed by Danny Siddons, whose green backpack dangled from one hand. It seemed weighty.

"Why, Jeremy," said Etta. "That's the first I've seen you wearing that shirt."

"We gave it to him for his birthday," Winnie explained. "We thought it would cheer him up."

Jeremy Braddock looked like somebody whose need to be cheered up was chronic. Juxtaposed with his sour face, the red shirt with its orange and turquoise flowers gave him the appearance of a tourist who'd been on one bus tour too many. He fidgeted with a large diamond ring on the pinky of one hand; then, when he saw the others watching him, he brought his puffy white hands to rest over the landscape of his belly and stared.

"Well?" he said at last.

Sebastian cleared his throat. "Um . . . well, Mr. Braddock, we thought . . . that is. . . ."

Jeremy waved a fat hand in the air impatiently. "Let the interview commence," he said. "Danny, sit down."

Danny did as he was told, making sure that he kept a grip on his backpack.

"If you don't want to be interviewed. . . ."

"Nonsense, young man. What makes you say that? Etta and Winnie told me of your idea and, despite some reluctance on Daniel's part here, I thought it first-rate. I'm not sure we'll have a lot to tell you, but we'll do our best. You . . . Barth, isn't it?"

"Yessir," said Sebastian, who was rarely intimidated by adults but found that this time he was.

Jeremy attempted a smile and said, "What is it you want to know?"

The interview lasted for almost thirty minutes, longer than Sebastian had expected it would. But given the many long pauses, there were probably no more than twenty minutes that could be used. Sebastian didn't really care one way or another; he was quite sure the interview would never be broadcast anyway.

Danny looked greatly relieved when Sebastian turned off the tape recorder and brought the interview to an end. He asked the Braddock sisters for a glass of water and proceeded to drink it down in one gulp.

"My, aren't you thirsty," said Etta to Danny. Then, chuckling, she turned to Winnie and said, "Remember what Mama used to say, Win?"

"Indeed I do," Winnie said. " 'You may quench a thirst, you may quench a fire. But you'll never quench the words of a liar.' "

Danny started to choke.

"He's swallowed the wrong way!" Jeremy exclaimed, showing more emotion than he had all afternoon. "Hit him on the back, Etta. For God's sake, don't just stand there like an old poop."

When they were back outside, David said to Sebastian, "Pretty interesting the way Danny choked when he did, huh? Guess he was lying, all right."

"No guessing about it. They were both lying through their teeth the whole time."

"What do you suppose Danny had in his backpack?" Corrie asked.

Sebastian was struggling to remember something he'd read in the newspaper recently—something about rare books. "Anything's possible," he said.

"So," said David, "what did you learn that you didn't know? Did the interview prove anything?"

"Yes," Sebastian said. He stopped and looked back at the Braddocks' house. "It proved that Danny's scared."

"Scared of what?"

"Scared of us. There was no way he was going to do this interview, remember? But somehow he let himself be convinced. And the only one I can see who has that kind of power over Danny is Jeremy Braddock. They're both scared . . . scared that we've found them out. And they've decided the best thing to do is play innocent." Sebastian paused and said, "Let's go back to your house, Corrie. There's a pretty good view of the church from the den, right?"

Corrie nodded. "But what—"

"You'll see."

Fifteen minutes later, the three watched as Danny Siddons entered First Church.

32

THEY KEPT WATCH all afternoon. When it was six o'clock and
they had seen no one else enter or
leave the church, they decided to call it quits.

Rather, it was decided for them.

"Dinner," Ginny Wingate called from the
kitchen.

"I gotta go anyway," David said. "I promised
Dad I'd be home by now. I have to, yuck, stay with
Rachel tonight."

"Josh going out?" Sebastian asked.

"Yeah, he's got a date. You want to come over?"

Sebastian hesitated. "I can't. There's some stuff
I need to do. Maybe I'll come over later, like ten."

"I wonder what Danny's been doing over there
all this time," Corrie said with a nod toward the
church.

"Maybe he's been catching up on his reading,"
David said.

After dinner that night, Sebastian went out the
kitchen door and cut across the back lawns of his
neighbors until he reached the corner of Chestnut
and Main. He didn't want David or Corrie to see

him. What he was about to do, he told himself, he had to do alone. He didn't want to endanger his friends.

He was thinking about Eric and remembering the last note he'd received from him as he ran across the green and swung back up to the side of First Church that faced away from Corrie's house. There he stopped to catch his breath. He was about to enter the church when he saw the door open; quickly, he tucked himself behind a large oak tree.

Danny Siddons, his face red and contorted, his hands clenched into fists, moved down the stairs and away from the church. Sebastian saw that his green backpack was hanging loosely from his shoulders, its weightiness gone. At the sidewalk's end, Danny stood for a moment, wiping his face with his hands. He glanced at his watch, then walked across the green and into the heart of town.

Sebastian's eyes followed him. Danny went into a pizza place. Sebastian saw by the clock on the church tower that it was a little after eight. It seemed that Danny was going to have dinner before returning to the church to ring the nine o'clock bell. There would be more than enough time to do what had to be done.

The air inside the church was cool and still. Sebastian filled his lungs with it as he climbed the stairs to the balcony and organ loft, then opened the door leading up to the bell tower. He listened as he entered the small vestibule at the tower stairs' base. He didn't hear a sound. As he'd expected, the stairway was dark. He reached into his pocket for the small flashlight he'd brought with him. He didn't notice the piece of paper that fell to the ground as he removed his hand.

Slowly, stealthily, he crept up the stairs. He heard the two stairs squeak before he came to the third. He did not need to step on it to know this was the one. He knelt down and gave the top of the stair a firm push with the heel of his hand. It came loose easily. Inside, by the light of the flashlight, a surprise met his eyes.

"Books!" he whispered. He hadn't been prepared for this.

He picked one up. Its brown leather cover was tattered and stained; the gold lettering on its front worn away. Sebastian opened it to its yellow-spotted title page. *Little Women*. He stared at it for a moment, puzzled. Was Jeremy Braddock dealing in rare books after all?

Suddenly, he remembered the story he'd read in the newspaper about some rare books being stolen from a library in New Haven. Could it be . . . ?

He set the book aside, picked up another. *The Complete Sherlock Holmes*. Its size belied its weight. It was odd how such a hefty book sat so lightly in his hand. He put it down and picked up a third—Stephen King's *Cujo*. He knew this was not an old book, let alone a rare one. What *was* Braddock up to, anyway? He looked back at the Sherlock Holmes. And then he realized.

Quickly, he reached for the large book. It did not take him long to find the hollowed out center. In it was a small package. He opened it and found what he'd been looking for. He knew from David's research what it was.

He was so engrossed in his discovery that he did not hear the stairs squeak. Nor did he hear the agitated breathing behind him until it was too late. He felt someone's hands grab his shoulders and give them a hard yank. As he began his swift descent down the stairs, he saw the flashlight drop and go out. In its final working moment, it illuminated a spray of something white flying through the air and down the stairs. Sebastian hit his head on the floor. For the briefest part of a second, he was aware of light coming in from a door nearby. Then the light was gone. And he was aware of nothing at all.

Lying beside his outstretched hand was the paper that had fallen from his pocket. It read:

Before the fall, a flash of white.
After the fall, black as night.

33

SOMEWHERE in his brain, Sebastian Barth was aware of being lifted under the arms and dragged some distance. His skin felt the air change as he was moved outside the church. He heard different sounds, smelled different smells. But he could make no sense of any of it. It all became a part of a twisted dream.

The ringing of the bell shattered the dream and returned him to a reality no less confusing. He looked around him. There was the church. But where was he?

He heard a low moan. He turned his head sharply and winced at the pain, then felt the bump on the back of his head. Suddenly, he remembered. The books. The sound of breathing. The pull on his shoulders. The flash of white. The fall.

There was another moan. He tried to stand and failed. He realized now that he'd been propped up against the small storage shed between the church and the cemetery. He turned his head again. Slowly this time.

Someone's silhouette was framed in the open back door of the Wingate house. It was Corrie. He watched her descend the porch stairs and enter the cemetery. He struggled to his feet. He was standing. Now all he had to do was walk.

As he put one foot in front of the other, feeling a little like Frankenstein's monster, he thought about what he'd seen in the church tower. He knew he had to confront Danny Siddons, but how? And when? Had the bell rung more than twice? Twice was all he recalled hearing. He turned back for a moment and looked at the church. The tower was lit. Danny was still up there.

"Corrie," he called out, turning back.

"Sebastian," said Corrie, seeing him come into the cemetery. "What are you doing here?"

"What are *you*?"

"I live here, remember? Next door, anyway. I just heard those moans again. Hey, what happened to you? You look kind of white."

"Somebody was trying to teach me a lesson," said Sebastian. "The kind I've never been too good at learning."

Corrie looked confused.

"The mind-your-own-business kind," Sebastian said by way of explanation.

Before Corrie could question him further, the moans from the grave turned into words. "Give me my ring," the voice said. "I want my ring."

Corrie shivered. "Spooky, huh?" she said.

"I think it's time we got to the bottom of this,"

Sebastian replied. He knelt down by Susan Siddons's gravestone and began to dig. It wasn't long before his fingernails scratched against a wire cage. Inside was a cassette tape recorder. "Just what I thought," he said.

"I can't believe it. Who would go to all the trouble—"

"Listen," Sebastian said, silencing her with an upraised hand. There was a rustling sound nearby. Then there were whispers.

"In that bush," Sebastian whispered to Corrie. He pointed, and the two of them made out a patch of white moving among the shadows. He motioned for Corrie to follow, and they moved on cat feet to the back of the cemetery.

When they were several yards away, there was a sudden commotion. The sound was of many birds taking flight but, of course, it wasn't birds but people. And there weren't many, there were only three. One of them was wearing a long black dress and a wide-brimmed hat.

And one white glove.

"After them!" Sebastian shouted. But as he began to run, his head started to swim. He felt himself falter and had to hold on to the fence to keep from falling. "I can't. . . ."

"I'll get them," Corrie called over her shoulder. "Or one of them, anyway," she said to herself.

She ran along the edge of the cemetery, across

her own backyard and into the yard next door. The person running ahead of her was slowed down by the long dress she was wearing. The other two were already out of sight. When Corrie gauged that she was close enough, she threw herself into the air and tackled her prey. They fell in a jumble. As they did, the black hat came off and the ghost's true identity was revealed.

"Janis!" Corrie exclaimed.

"Ta-da!" said Janis with a nervous laugh.

"It's *not* funny. You've really been scaring me. What's this all about, anyway?"

Janis looked completely flustered. She didn't say anything, just pursed her lips and raised and lowered her eyebrows.

"It's all right, Janis," a voice said. Corrie turned. It was Sebastian. "We know Ricky put you and your friends up to it."

"We do?"

"Ricky?"

"To throw us off the track. So we wouldn't figure out what Eric knew. But it's too late, Janis. I understand everything now. The only question left is what to do about it."

"What are you talking about?" Janis said, sitting up and dusting herself off. "What does Ricky have to do with anything?"

"Don't play innocent. Eric knew what was going on with Danny, right? He broke his leg because of it and was afraid to say anything. But he decided to send me clues so I'd try to figure it out. Before he moved, he must have told you what he was going to do. Why, I'm not sure. But you told Ricky. And Ricky made sure you let him know what Eric's clues were. In fact, he suggested you help Eric out. That way, he'd make sure the clues all sounded as if they had to do with the ghost instead of . . . instead of what they really had to do with."

"I hate to burst your bubble," Janis said, "but Ricky has nothing to do with this."

"He doesn't?"

Janis shook her head.

"Honest?"

"Honest, Sebastian. Doesn't Ricky have enough problems without a ghost to worry about?"

Sebastian nodded. "He sure does," he said.

The bell of First Church rang once, then fell silent.

"I've got to go," Sebastian said. He started walking away.

Janis stood. "Hey," she said, "can you give me a hand first?"

"What do you mean?" Sebastian asked.

"My tape recorder. Can you help me get it out?"

Sebastian regarded the church with a worried look. "I guess so," he said. "But let's hurry."

As they were digging, Sebastian remarked to Corrie, "By the way, that rubber hose?"

"Yes?"

"It's running from that bush over there." He picked up the end lying behind the stone. "Handy way to make smoke rise up out of a grave, don't you think? The thing I *don't* understand is why the hoax. If Ricky wasn't behind it, it must have been Eric. But why? What *did* he know?"

Janis smiled. "I guess that's just one more mystery for you to solve," she said.

"Sebastian," Corrie said softly. Her fingers were running along part of the gravestone that had been submerged below the earth. "There's writing here. See?"

By the light of the moon, they were able to make out the words, "My husband Cornelius."

Sebastian studied this new discovery for a moment, then lifted his eyes to the epitaph. Something was becoming clear. And it might just provide what he needed to deal with Danny.

The bell rang again. Sebastian rose and, with slow, deliberate steps, walked to the church.

34 THE VOICES Sebastian heard coming from the tower seemed beyond
the point of caring if anyone heard.
They were loud, and they were angry. And they were
as filled with passion as a snake is filled with venom.

Sebastian crept up the tower stairs, careful to
avoid those steps that would betray him, and
shrouded himself in the darkness at the top. In the
dim light before him, he saw Danny grab Ricky by
the arms.

"You don't get it, do you?" Danny was saying.
Ricky tried to push his brother away. "I'm in big
trouble now."

"You've been in big trouble for a long time,"
Ricky said. He succeeded in throwing Danny off and
stood rubbing his arms.

"Not like this," Danny said. His voice shook.
"Not like this. Do you have any idea how much that
stuff you spilled all over the stairs is worth?"

"I told you. I didn't spill it. Sebastian—"

"Sebastian, Sebastian. What are you blaming him
for? If you hadn't grabbed him, he wouldn't have

tossed that bag, and I wouldn't be out a few thousand dollars worth of—"

"Danny, Sebastian *knows*. I got scared. I . . . I didn't know what else to do! All I knew was that he'd found you out. When I saw him there, I just kind of went crazy. I didn't know what he'd do. So I grabbed him. I didn't mean for him to pass out like that. Then I dragged him outside and—"

"Bright, kid," said Danny. "Real bright. What's he gonna do when he comes to? And what if you really hurt him? Your kind of help I can do without!" Danny started pacing, puffing out his cheeks and wiping his forehead with the back of his hand.

No one said anything. Then Ricky hunkered down against a wall and crossed his arms over his knees. Finally, he spoke. "Sebastian's smart, Danny. He's going to put it all together. Then what?"

"What do you care?" Danny spat out. "You're ready to turn me in anyway, aren't you? Turn in your own brother."

Ricky's voice trembled when he answered. "I don't want to, Danny. I don't want to. But I can't keep watching you do this to yourself. You just keep getting in deeper and deeper. And one of these days—"

"One of these days, what?"

Ricky looked up at his brother. There were tears in his eyes. His lower lip quivered. If he had an answer to Danny's question, he could not get it out.

Danny looked away.

Again, there was a long silence. And again, it was Ricky who broke it.

"I used to look up to you,"he said in a soft voice. He managed to keep back his tears, but his lip still quivered. "I used to think you were the greatest thing going. My big brother. And then . . . you changed. When you didn't get into all those fancy colleges and Dad was getting on your case, you started staying out a lot. Last year, I could tell you were messing around with drugs. You just weren't the same. And things weren't the same with us. You weren't my big brother anymore. You were just another bummed-out druggie."

Danny was still looking away from his brother. "Maybe that's who I really am," he said. "Maybe I'm just a druggie. And maybe I'm happy being that. I'm not as smart as Dad, you know. Or you."

"Nobody said you had to be."

"Oh, yeah?" Danny said, turning to face Ricky. "So why'd they cut off my money when my grades slipped last year, huh? Because it's a family disgrace to be anything but an A student. Even if you *don't* go to Harvard. It's a family disgrace to be anything but the best. Well, I'm *not* the best, Ricky. And I'm tired of trying. I'm tired of trying."

"So who expects you to be the best?"

"Everybody," Danny said simply. "Dad. Mother.

You. Everybody here in Pembroke. Everybody at school. I'm a Siddons, right? And I'm the oldest. I'm supposed to be smart like Dad, good like Dad, a saint like Dad. And not just *Dad*. Every Siddons back to Cornelius. Cornelius!" Danny snorted. "The man haunts us all. The man who put Pembroke on the map; the man who founded a college; the man who gave half his fortune to charities; the man who—"

"The man who murdered his wife," said Sebastian Barth, stepping from the shadows.

Danny started. "How long have you been there?"

"Long enough. But, don't worry, Danny. I didn't hear anything I didn't already know."

"What'd you say about Cornelius?" Ricky said.

"He murdered his wife Susan. There's proof." Sebastian turned to Danny. "So Cornelius wasn't a saint after all. Maybe once people know that, they won't expect you to be."

Danny's surprise at Sebastian's news was short-lived. "Cornelius is dead," he said fiercely. "But I've got a life to live. And I'm not having it ruined by a couple of nosy kids."

Sebastian said, "Me and Eric, huh?"

"Who's talking about Eric?" said Danny. "He didn't know anything about all this. I'm talking about you and Ricky. Why do you have to snoop around where you don't belong, anyway?"

Sebastian shrugged. "I'm curious," he said. "I was trying to solve one mystery and it led me to another. I started out looking for a ghost. But I found you, Danny. You're all messed up on cocaine, and once your parents cut off your allowance, you started pushing the stuff for Jeremy Braddock. I'm not sure why, but you've been using the church bell as a code to let the dealers in the area know where a drop was being made."

"How do you know so much?"

"I have a friend who does a lot of reading. Besides, I have eyes and I have ears. And I use them."

Ricky looked at Sebastian in astonishment; then he dropped his head between his hands. Danny watched him.

"That's why *I* was snooping around," Sebastian said. "I think you know why Ricky was. Whatever he says, you're still his big brother."

Ricky's breathing turned jagged as the tears he'd been holding back broke loose.

Danny didn't say anything. He watched Ricky. His mouth began to lose its hardness. His shoulders slackened. After a time he walked to his brother and knelt down beside him.

Reaching out to touch him on the shoulder, he said, "I'm sorry, kid." But Ricky pulled away.

Danny kept his hand suspended between them. When he turned his face to Sebastian, he looked tired and confused. And he looked old. His eyes asked Sebastian to understand.

After a moment, he stood up, crossed the small

room, and bent down to pick up his green backpack.

In a hollow voice, he said, "Let's go."

Twenty minutes later, Sebastian, Danny, and Ricky walked into the Pembroke police station. Alex was working late that night.

"What's up, fellas?" he asked.

"You know Danny Siddons, don't you, Alex?"

Alex nodded.

"Well," Sebastian said, "he has something he wants to tell you."

35 THE NEXT DAY, Tuesday, Katie Hallem took her son to the doctor. He was given a clean bill of health and told to watch his step.

On Wednesday, Sebastian and David taped that week's "Small Talk." The interview with Jeremy Braddock and Danny Siddons was not used. Instead, the topic was "Should Girls Play Football?" One of the guests was Corrie Wingate.

36

"IT TOOK four men to lift that stone. And I can't tell you the support that's needed to keep it there," Jessica said.

She rested her hand in the crook of Sebastian's elbow. Corrie and David stood on either side of them. Together, they gazed up at the gravestone, now hanging on the wall of the Pembroke Historical Society.

SUSAN IRIS SIDDONS

DIED

AUGUST 10. 1902.

AGED 49 YEARS.

In life did I reap much pain,
In death greater pain I sow.
'Tis a garden of poison'd ivy,
And the roots lie here below.

———

My husband Cornelius,
Together with my nurse Jenny Webster,
Did conspire to murder me

[129]

By administering doses of poison
With my nightly medicine.

My daughter Elvira was
Witness to this sad truth.

"I always thought that was strange," said Sebastian, pointing to the words, *poison'd ivy*. "But I figured it was just an old-fashioned way of saying poison ivy."

"So did we all," Jessica remarked. "Alas, even when I learned that Susan Siddons's real middle name was Ivy, I didn't put two and two together."

"I never even thought about it," Corrie confessed.

"I didn't think about it either," said Sebastian, "at first. It wasn't until I saw the words 'My husband Cornelius' that night that it really clicked. If she was saying she'd been poisoned and the roots were down below, well, then it made sense that she was naming her murderer. Anyway, it was a hunch."

"And it paid off," David said. He looked at his friend and shook his head. "Somehow, with you, it always does."

"Yes," said Jessica, letting go of her grandson's arm and seating herself at an eighteenth-century writing desk. "And because of your discovery, the Siddons family has come forward and revealed that they've known the truth all along. It was a family secret passed along to each new generation at the age of twenty-one. A shame that Danny hadn't known. Perhaps it would have helped." She opened a drawer and pulled out a torn, yellowed sheet of paper. "The missing page from Elvira's diary," she said, holding it up. "She describes in detail how her father and Jenny Webster poisoned her mother over a period of months. Unfortunately, she came upon the truth too late to save her mother. And, fearing that her father's position in the community would protect him from any accusations she might make, she said nothing. She kept her dark secret, sharing it with her sisters and brothers only after her father's death years later. Yet, in her own way, she made her secret known to anyone who would see. For it was she who had the gravestone carved."

Jessica replaced the paper in the drawer. "It's a sad day for Pembroke," she said.

"It's a sad day for the Siddonses," said Sebastian.

Jessica nodded. "That, too," she said. "That, too."

"I wonder what's going to happen to Danny," said Corrie.

"Oh, don't worry about him," David said. "He's rich. He'll get off easy."

Jessica scowled. "I don't know about that," she said. "I don't think the Siddons family wields quite the influence it once did. Besides, he committed a serious crime, David. That's not to be taken lightly.

One can only hope that the judge will be merciful. What Danny did was wrong, very wrong. But he did it out of a great deal of anguish and confusion. And who among us has not had his moments of anguish and confusion?"

For a moment, no one spoke but the clocks. When the grandfather chimed, Jessica sighed and said, "I guess there will be no more bells at nine o'clock." Then, turning to Sebastian, she said, "You know, I still don't understand how you did it."

"Did what?"

"Determined that Danny was involved in the drug trade."

"Well," said Sebastian, easing himself down onto a carpeted platform, "I didn't really know what was going on at first. I just knew that Danny was acting strange. The first real clue I had was that dollar bill we found in the tower."

"This one?" David asked, pulling a bill from his wallet.

"It didn't look like that when you found it," Sebastian said. "It was curled up, remember?"

David cocked his head to the side. "So?"

"Well, I didn't think anything of it until Corrie said that it might have been Danny's. Then I remembered hearing that rolled-up paper money was sometimes used to snort cocaine. From that point on, I was watching Danny through different eyes. After we followed him that night, it didn't take me long to figure out he was working with Jeremy Braddock.

"According to Alex, Jeremy was a very big distributor of drugs in this area. Danny was his go-between. He used the nine o'clock bell as a code to let the other dealers know where to meet him to get their drugs. Because Danny and Jeremy didn't trust using their phones, they invented the bell code. Besides, Jeremy was an invalid and couldn't get out. He wanted to know when and where a drop was being made."

"And then Sebastian had me do some reading for him," said David.

"Danny kept talking about his 'girl,' but we knew from Ricky that he didn't have a girlfriend," Sebastian said. "Well, David found out that 'girl' is one of the nicknames for cocaine."

"And the shut-in society?" asked Jessica.

"Just a cover to fool the Braddock sisters," Sebastian replied.

Jessica shook her head. "You're quite a detective," she told her grandson. "I shall have to remember to keep my doors locked."

"Oh, I'm not *such* a detective," Sebastian said.

The others looked at him.

"I still haven't figured out what Eric knew," he said.

37

AFTER LEAVING the historical society, Sebastian, Corrie, and David headed in the direction of Katie's restaurant.

"I need a banana cooler," David said. "It must be ninety-five degrees today."

Sebastian was lost in thought.

"Eric's notes must have been about the ghost, after all," he said at last. "Even that last one. The flash of white was supposed to be the white glove—you know, Susan Siddons before she pushed him down the stairs. I really don't think he knew anything about what was going on with Danny."

"And Ricky wasn't in on Eric's thing, either," said David.

Sebastian agreed. "I think he knew about it, but he was so worried about Danny he didn't want any part of it."

"Janis has admitted that she and a couple of her friends helped Eric plan the whole thing," Corrie said. "She even wrote those notes before he moved."

"So it was all a put-on." David sighed.

"Yeah," said Corrie. "To tell you the truth, I'm

a little disappointed. I was getting used to the idea of living next door to a ghost. I even kind of liked it. It was more fun than living in Troy, anyway."

"We'll do our best to keep life exciting for you," Sebastian said with a smile.

Corrie smiled back. Then she said, "The only thing I don't understand is Uncle Harry's story. Did he really see a ghost or what?"

Sebastian sighed. "I'm afraid Gram's right about Uncle Harry. He loves a good story."

"His dog was probably barking at a shadow or a statue or something," said David, "and Uncle Harry filled in the rest."

"I'll bet you knew all along it was a put-on, didn't you?" Corrie said to Sebastian then.

"Well, I guess I did. The thing that really clinched it, though, was the ring." He extracted a tissue from his pocket, unfolded it and pulled a gold ring from its center. "Look inside," he said to Corrie and David.

"S.I.S.," said David. "Is there something else we're supposed to see?"

Sebastian shook his head. "Isn't that enough?"

"I don't get it," said Corrie.

"If Cornelius Siddons had given his second wife his first wife's ring, don't you think he would have removed her initials first?"

"Huh!" David said. "I wonder where the ring came from, then."

[135]

"Probably out of a gumball machine," said Sebastian, putting it back in his pocket. "What *I* wonder is why the put-on. Was Eric just playing with us? Or was he covering up something else? And why did he fall down the stairs?"

When they opened the door of Harvest Home, a surprise greeted them.

"Mrs. Mather!"

"Well, hello, Sebastian. Hello, David. And you must be Corrie. I've been hearing all about you and your . . . exploits."

Katie smiled at the kids. "This is Mrs. Mather, Corrie," she said. "She used to live in your house."

"She's Eric's mom," David whispered, which was more to the point.

"What are you doing here?" Sebastian asked.

Katie looked surprised at her son's question.

"I mean, it's nice to see you. But . . . say, did Eric come with you?"

Mrs. Mather laughed. "I had to go into Hartford for something, Sebastian. I just thought I'd swing by this way and say hello to your mother. And, no, Eric didn't come with me."

"Mrs. Mather," Sebastian said in a tentative way, "did Eric . . . has Eric said anything to you about a ghost?"

Mrs. Mather laughed again. This time, Katie joined her. "We were just talking about that," Mrs. Mather said. "I'm sorry for laughing. It's really not funny. I know I'm not supposed to say anything to you, but, well, enough is enough. Eric made that whole thing up just to keep you boys on your toes. He decided you needed a good mystery to solve after he was gone. Personally, I thought it was a little cruel ... particularly as it involved Corrie. But he and his girlfriend thought it was quite a hoot."

"His what?" said David.

"His girlfriend," Eric's mother said. "You know Janis Tupper, don't you?"

"I don't believe it," Sebastian said, slapping his thigh. "Janis has been two-timing Ricky with Eric. Is that why he was acting so weird before you moved?"

"He was in love. The poor boy was walking around in a daze. That's how he came to fall down the cellar stairs." Mrs. Mather put her hand to her mouth. "I think I've said more than I should have. Eric didn't really want you two to know. He said he would never have heard the end of it if you'd known he had a girlfriend. Let's just say this is our little secret, shall we?" And she winked at them.

"Sure, Mrs. Mather," said Sebastian. And he winked back.

"If you kids want to wash up, I've just baked some terrific whole wheat brownies," Katie said. "What do you say?"

In the men's room, David said, "I can't believe it. Eric fell down the stairs because of a *girl*. I'll tell you what he knew, Sebastian—girls mean trouble! That's what Eric knew."

Sebastian thought of Danny then. "I think," he said, "that it depends on the 'girl.' "

"Hey, listen," David said, as they went back into the dining room, "you want to come over to my house tonight?"

"I can't. I've got plans."

"Plans? What kind of plans?"

"Well, I guess you'd call it a date."

"A date?" David said. "Like, with a girl?"

Sebastian smiled.

"Sebastian. . . ." David said.

"What do you want to do tonight?" Sebastian asked Corrie as he sat down beside her.

"Roller-skating?" Corrie suggested.

"Sebastian!"

Sebastian looked up at David.

"What does this mean?" David asked.

In a whisper, Sebastian said, "Maybe when you're thirteen, you'll find out."

David sank into a chair and reached for a brownie. "Mister Enigmatic," he muttered.